Sisters' Homecoming

Clark Family Legend, Book 6

by
Richard E Friesen

1
CHANGE OF PLANS

The meandering spaceport on Planeta de Angel seemed strange now, after spending time in Beijing and Launching City where things had been built with a purpose and a plan. I stepped out the door of Earl's shop and stopped. There on the left, a row of windows looked out over the Precipice, a stunning view of a steaming lake bordered by sharp ridges that kept the lava flows out of the water and the roiling methane atmosphere. And yet, no one came out to see it. The only people to make it this far needed to talk to Earl, the best ship mechanic on the planet, about something wrong on their starship.

With a snort of amusement at the idea of being the first "tourist" in this corridor, I strode inward toward the main terminal, turning left, then right, and right again. I passed airlock doors leading to docking berths. I'd had one of those once, could have again, but I wasn't staying long, and Earl, my starship mechanic and maybe friend, was fine parking my ship, the now famous and unique *Hiram's Revenge* in his shop. An ordinary small freighter with a hatch on the rear of the personnel deck on top and a ramp up to the cargo bay, and painted black of course, with no markings. It appeared normal from the inside, too, but it wasn't.

This trip into the domed town of Puerto Fronterizo, I intended to see some old friends, so I'd strapped my plasma pistol on for the first time in over a year.

I'd left from here to go pick up Ambassador Retts on Eksil and take her to Earth, which resulted in showing off how *Hiram's Revenge* could maneuver in Lu Space, which no other ship could do, yet. Our little adventure had gotten Eksil added to the Council of Planets and brought down the president of said council, when it came out that he'd conspired to stop us.

The only reason I'd come back was that Earl had wanted to come home. While on Thurman after leaving Ambassador Retts on Earth, Earl and I, along with my lawyer, Abraham Stone, had negotiated a lucrative contract with Pauley Spaceways. Both of us were set for life. Together we'd changed the way hyper-jumps in Lu space could be done, and in addition to a few hundred million up front we would get half a percent of each ship sold with our modifications. Flying Earl back here myself seemed like the least I could do.

When the familiar spaceport scents of hydraulic oil and warm electronics, plus the whine of gravity drives and the hubbub of people coming and going reached my senses, a smile broke on my face. I was a freelance pilot, and this was familiar territory. The windows at the docks that were in use were frosted or blacked out. Only the empty ones had clear windows, which also explained the winding corridors; none of those windows showed a ship in dock.

I reached the Lava Grill with its red and orange décor and a mix of tourists trying to get used to this strange place and ship's crews waiting to come or go. It served wonderful pulled pork garnished with pineapple, but their cookies were even better.

By then, I was starting to *feel* like a freelancer again.

Beyond the grill were shops selling contraband, or what was contraband elsewhere, a drug shop selling hallucinogens, a tech shop with hacking hardware and software, and a brothel boasting zero-g rooms with backdrops of a hundred planets.

When I reached the vaulted walkway between the spaceport and the domed city of Puerto Fronterizo, I stepped to the side and watched. I'd spent almost five years flying in and out of here in my exile. After this trip, I doubted I'd be back, although I didn't know what I *would* do. I still didn't have a home, other than *Hiram's Revenge*. Conrad Maeda, my old boss at Pauley Spaceways Special Projects, would probably hire me back, but that wasn't for me. Maybe some small engineering firm, but I'd miss flying *Hiram's Revenge*. It was also time for me to move out of Kaia's place. It had been nice living with my chatterbox college roommate again for a few months, but I needed to find or make my *own* home.

Just the thought created a hollowness in my chest and a darkness in my soul. I'd gotten away from the bastards who'd created me, at least mostly. But how did one go about making a home? A life? Go back and steal Hiram from his wife? That just seemed wrong.

With a shake of the head, I pushed off and headed through the vaulted corridor and into Puerto Fronterizo, now showing pyramids from Chichén Itzá in Mexico on the walls between the windows.

When I reached the end of the tunnel, I turned left at the first cross street, walking past the little shops that sold stolen software and cleaning robots, and others selling boring clothes or groceries.

I stepped up to the counter at Marta's empanada place and leaned on it. I did not recognize the young woman ready to take my order.

Smiling, I held up three fingers. "Today's special, tres, and a horchata. I'm Deuce, and I'd like to talk to Marta."

She served me the empanadas and a drink with a smile and went to the back to find Marta.

When Marta stepped out into the restaurant and saw me, she rushed around the counter and gave me a hug. "Deuce! We thought you were dead!"

I held her at arm's length. "No, just learning how to end my exile. Still not sure I've figured it out."

Someone called out, "Burgundy!"

I ignored him. No one knew that name here. Marta scowled, not pleased with what she saw.

The same voice, somewhat quieter, said, "Deuce! I need you."

Furious, I turned, sluggish and calculated to annoy. I found Admiral Jackson, retired, striding toward me with four men in tow; hired muscle. Jackson had been my sister

Brandy's commanding officer in the Nova Roman war, and my workout partner or something like that at the Clark Academy. What the hell was *he* doing here? And how dare he use my real name! Marta would figure it out for sure.

One of Jackson's thugs had a big, black mustache. Another had a black eye. The third had long blond hair, and the fourth was a woman with a bodybuilder's muscles. What a motley crew.

Jackson stepped right up to Marta and me. "Walk with me."

I rolled my eyes at Marta, then shook my head and walked down the road with Jackson.

Once out of earshot from Marta, Jackson pitched his voice low. "I'm staging a rescue, and I need to hire a pilot for the escape. I was just headed to the Abogada, but this job is made for you."

I stopped and put my hands on my hips. "Then my price just tripled."

Jackson raised an eyebrow, then nodded with a grin. "Done."

He held out a hand for me to shake.

Oh, hell. If he would do that without a thought, this was dangerous and difficult. But I hadn't said quintuple, which I apparently should have. He always seemed like he knew more than he was letting on. Still, he had helped me back at the Clark Academy and had been a friend of my sister Brandy for years. I wasn't sure I owed him anything, but he was an old friend.

I shook his hand, and we started off. I'd intended to go get a drink from Ramon, the bartender at the Abogada. I turned to wave at Marta. "Tell Ramon and the gang at the Abogada that I'm still alive." I gave Jackson a glare. "For now."

She winked at me, but her eyes darting to the thugs expressed her worry. "I will."

I fell in line beside Jackson and pitched my voice low. "What the hell?"

He snorted. "Frankly, I was lucky you were here. I've been living here a few months and got word a spy was kidnapped. We need to get him back."

Why did I think luck had nothing to do with it? And what did a retired admiral have to do with spies? Still, I used my bracer to send a quick message to Earl. "Get the *Revenge* ready to fly. Leaving sooner than expected."

And suddenly, without trying, I was in deep—deeper than I wanted or needed. "That brings up nineteen more questions. Where are we flying?"

He hesitated. "Thurman."

I hadn't planned to go back to my home planet, but I didn't have anywhere else to go either. Still, this sounded less and less good. I shook my head as we walked. "I should have asked for ten times my rate."

Jackson laughed.

When we reached the main road, we turned away from the spaceport, deeper into Puerto Fronterizo.

As we walked, a realization struck me. In other places, like Beijing, you could tell the good and bad neighborhoods by the shabbiness of the houses and how well places were maintained, even if humble. Not in a place like Angel's Planet. Nothing here was more than twenty years old, most less than ten. And all of it had been constructed with the same giant printers, using the same raw materials. The buildings had charcoal gray walls with blue and orange highlights.

Near the center of town, Jackson led us left again, into a neighborhood I did not know. The buildings rose two or three stories above us, making a gray canyon with shops below and apartments above, some with balconies. The canyons grew tighter and darker when Jackson cut through an alleyway. No windows broke the walls there, just a few emergency doors above us that would extrude their own stairs or ladders if needed.

At last, the alley expanded into a little open-air market that had food and recreational drugs sold side-by-side, and which opened to a normal street on the far side. The only similar market I'd been to sold clothes and hacking tools. Here, tourists and locals lounged on chairs eating and getting high.

We crossed the market, weaving between chairs and vendor's carts, and stopped by the next street. There, Jackson gathered us. "He's in room three-seventeen in that hotel across the street." He pointed at Mustache Thug. "Get to the roof, make sure they don't have anyone up there. Then let us know if anyone else comes in."

Mustache stroked his facial hair, tapped his ear, and headed out and went left up the street a bit before crossing.

Jackson turned back with a grin. "I'm hungry. Let's get something to eat."

We went back and got some kabobs and watched people getting high. The food-cart vendor had spiced the vat-grown meat well. I savored every bite.

It only took a few minutes before Jackson cocked his head. "Scout on the roof eliminated. Now we walk in the front door like we belong."

That's when I noticed they had earbuds. Belatedly, I dashed after Jackson and his thugs as they crossed the street.

I elbowed him. "When do I get an earbud?"

Jackson ignored me.

Walking into the hotel lobby was like walking into a nudist beach in San Tropez. The room had a gorgeous cove displayed on three walls, with beach chairs and real sand trickling onto the floors. On those lounge chairs reclined four men and three women, naked and available for various services. A massage—a real one for stiff muscles—sounded good about now. Of course, I didn't need to buy services when I could afford to buy the whole brothel. If I wanted to.

Jackson didn't even pause, though his thugs cast lingering gazes.

There was an elevator in the hallway off the main lobby, but Jackson trotted up the stairs next to it. The stairway was utilitarian, printed like the exterior walls but with slip-proof treads added. Again, I brought up the rear.

By the time I reached the third floor, the others had already gone out into the hall and the metal door was swinging shut. I slipped through into a corridor with black carpet speckled with the same blues as the gray walls. Ten meters down, I saw Jackson and the long-haired thug flanking the near side of the door for three-seventeen, with bodybuilder and shiner standing on the other side. None of them stood directly in front of the opening.

I warmed up my plasma pistol.

Hairy, whose tresses made me jealous, pulled out a small electronic device. I arrived just as Jackson reached over to knock. locks

Someone answered from inside. Jackson spoke with a thick accent. Then four shots punched through the door.

Hairy held his device to the lock. The door popped open. Shiner drew a firearm, pushed the door open, and dove in. The wall on the far side told me the room extended my direction.

Shots came at a sharp angle. From someone standing beside the door. The thugs fired back.

Gambling where the shoot was, I turned and fired through the wall. The plasma blasted through the thin printed internal wall.

Then I hit the carpet. Shots flew out the hole I'd made. Hairy and Bodybuilder launched through the door. Two shots and a couple thuds followed.

One of the thugs called, "All clear!"

Jackson and I went in. A regular hotel room with smart walls, the ceiling set to mirror and the walls to some park. The bed had hooks designed for tying up guests. Shiner-thug was on the ground, writhing in pain. Two strangers lay on the carpet, one bleeding, one moaning. A woman lay tied to the bed.

Assuming the one on the bed was the one we'd come to rescue, I dashed over and untied her.

She sat up, rubbing her wrists. "Who the hell are you idiots?"

I leaned close so the thugs wouldn't hear. "That's Admiral Jackson, who commanded the 14th in the war."

At that moment, Jackson, who'd knelt to put a pressure bandage on Shiner's wound, cocked his head. "We have visitors." Then he pointed at Hairy. "You change clothes with her. The three of you go to the bus terminal and buy tickets for Volcan Diablo. Then go to the women's room and change clothes again. Hurry!"

The woman on the bed had started to strip already. She showed no modesty at all.

Hairy scowled until Jackson offered to double his pay. Then he stripped and donned the woman's clothes.

The woman in thug clothing stopped to search through the pants of her bleeding captor to retrieve a data crystal, which she stuffed into her own pants. "Let's go."

Jackson sent Hairy and Bodybuilder dragging the wounded Shiner to the elevator. The rest of us went down the stairs. At the bottom, Jackson peeked through the door, then waited. At last, he signaled us, and we trooped back through the lobby and out under the dome.

We met Mustache back in the little market area, and headed out in a diamond, Mustache out front and our quarry in back, pretending to be a bodyguard so he could deal with any threats. I noticed she did a good job checking our surroundings.

At last, we reached the vaulted passage back to the spaceport. Then I felt safer, though this was a place we had to go, so someone might set an ambush here.

I stepped a little closer to Jackson in our diamond formation. "What the hell is this?"

"She's a spy with important information the Romans don't want the Council of Planets to get. Those guys who had her were hired to kidnap her on Tanterra, which has some laws the Romans didn't want to openly cross."

It made sense for them to bring a kidnap victim here to Angel's Planet, since no one here would care. It was the sort of thing Angel himself made sure no one cared about; he owned the whole planet. And I could get her to Thurman or even Earth faster than anyone but a courier.

When I wondered what I would do now that I had money, this hadn't been one of the choices.

We made it out of the tunnel into the terminal building. No ambush.

Still, I guided Mustache past the spaceport shops, around to the Lava Grill and through the winding corridors way out to the end. This time I walked right past the windows showing the Precipice and the roiling sky.

Earl's shop was the last door in the spaceport, where the corridor ended. Nothing lay beyond. From the windows, you could also see the shop extending out over the precipice. The floor there tilted down to let ships in and out. Since *Hiram's Revenge* was inside, Earl had given me access. The door had a sign that read *Earl Cristo, Starship Mechanic*.

I'd spent weeks with Earl building new Lu Space controls for *Hiram's Revenge* and selling the invention to Pauley Spaceways, and I'd yet to see any sign of a personality. His robot dog, Roberre, who could be playful, tender, and imposing had more personality.

The door recognized me, so I pulled it open and held it for Mustache.

We trooped into the front office, a room with smooth surfaces, a counter, and a door to the shop, which stood as an open invitation to enter. Since no one was in the front office, we headed on into the shop. I wondered where Roberre was. Usually, he met strangers right at the door.

Someone moved beside the doorway. A shot rang out.

2
HIT SQUAD

Hiram's Revenge shone black on Earl's shop floor. The ramp was down. Tools surrounded it. Earl was nowhere to be seen.

Sharp reports echoed from the high ceiling. Blood splattered. Mustache Thug crumpled.

I dropped to the ground and drew my pistol. Someone kicked my hand. It erupted in pain. My pistol skittered across the floor.

Jackson grunted. Everything got quiet. Someone wrenched my hands behind my back and locked them tight. They hauled me up and set me down on my feet, hard.

I stumbled. The hands didn't let me fall, but they twisted my arm. Then I saw. Mustache had a hole in his head, bleeding all over Earl's clean floor. I glanced out into the front office. The spy lay still in a similar pool of blood. Damn. A bullet had gone past my head. I would have been dead if they'd wanted me dead. Oh, shit. They thought the spy was a bodyguard, which meant they thought I was the spy.

Jackson, with a bruise on the side of his head, was being held by a young man with dark hair and vaguely Asian features.

Hiram's Revenge hadn't moved. The two doors across the way stood open on Earl's machine shop and parts room. Half the floor was empty, over on the side by the precipice, where the floor opened to let ships in from the bottom.

Fear settled in my belly, worse than any time flying freelance or at the academy. I'd just gotten out of exile. It couldn't end this way. But what could I do? I wasn't a soldier. I was an engineer. Tears stung my eyes.

Jackson held my gaze, as if to say more than his words. "Well, that didn't go as planned."

The person holding Jackson gave him a shake. "Quiet!"

Jackson rolled his eyes and made a face.

Before anyone could react—before I could laugh—a new voice cut the air. "Get those two out of the way. Get the bodies in here, and lock both doors."

A woman with a rifle walked down the *Revenge*'s ramp, pushing Earl ahead of her. Had she used *Hiram's Revenge* as a perch? The angle was right.

I wanted to punch her.

Earl, hands tied behind his back, walked as calmly as ever, but there was something in his eyes, an intense focus I had not seen before. I looked again and thought I'd imagined it. His face was so passive.

The two men pushed us against the wall and made us sit. Earl joined us, and the woman with the rifle kept watch. The two guys dragged the spy's body into the shop. Then they found mops and cleaned up some of the blood. Last, they closed and locked the door between the front office and the shop.

There was one person, well not really a person, missing: Roberre. Where was Roberre? And had Earl given Roberre weapons or not?

Earl squirmed a bit, probably upset about what was going on in his shop. I was numb now. The sight of the dead bodies did nothing to me at all. Maybe the fear had banished the horror and revulsion. It was just too much.

Then another thought came to me. They would *not* get my ship. No one took *Hiram's Revenge* from me. They'd taken Hiram, they could not have his ship. I'd blow it up first.

I stopped and blinked. I did have something I could do. They hadn't taken my bracer, which had remote control capabilities. And voice activation.

Could I let Jackson and Earl know? Maybe, assuming these idiots really thought I was the spy. "It's too bad we lost our pilot. Flying that ship could be useful."

Jackson leaned his head back against the wall. "True. Timing is everything. If we'd gotten back here sooner..."

Now if I could get them to take us near the ship.

The woman gestured to one of her men. "Get her up."

The guy grabbed me under the arms and lifted me to my feet. I want to bite him. Instead, I imitated Earl, passive and calm. I ended up facing the *Revenge*. Was that movement up on the ramp? I gave my attention to the woman before anyone noticed.

She came over and lifted my chin. "Where is the data crystal?"

I frowned, considering my clothes, and then told the truth. "Um...I think I left it in my other pants."

The woman slapped me. "Where is it?"

I wanted to rub my cheek. "Wait. I think I left it back at the hotel where those goons had me." I turned to Jackson. "Did I grab a data crystal before we left?"

He pursed his lips. "Hmm. No, I don't think you did. Which one of them had it?"

I scowled, even though this banter was kind of fun. "The dead one, I think. I really don't like touching dead bodies."

The woman stared up at the roof. "Why me?" Then she pointed her rifle at Jackson. "If you don't tell me where it is, I'll shoot the old man."

A glance at Jackson was all I could manage. Then again if I was the spy... "Him? I just met him half an hour ago."

She leaned close. "Stop messing around or everyone dies."

I considered biting her, shoving, something, but that would likely get me killed. Instead, I whispered in her ear. "I told you, it's in my other pants."

The woman grabbed my throat. "Then where are your other pants?"

It couldn't be that simple, could it? I rolled my eyes. "We sent my luggage ahead with Earl, of course. The pants are on board already."

The woman scowled, then motioned to her accomplices. "Get them up. We all go." To me she said, "Any funny stuff and the old man dies."

The woman moved around behind me while the men got Earl and Jackson to their feet. Then, with me in front, we headed toward the ramp.

Just as we reached the bottom, a loud bark echoed from above. Roberre charged down at me. Or maybe the woman.

The woman leapt to the side. She brought her gun to bear.

Just the distraction I needed. "*Revenge* on. Zero. Extend."

The *Revenge* whined. Roberre leaped. Gravity vanished.

A shimmer spread from the ship, marking where it had erased the planet's pull. Earl and Jackson were outside it. The woman and I were inside.

Earl twisted, blood on one wrist, hands free. Jackson jerked backwards. I jumped and tucked. Then twisted in midair.

Someone grabbed my foot. The woman had jumped after me.

Earl spun and grabbed his captor. He twisted the man's neck. It snapped.

Roberre hit Jackson's man in the chest. Dog and Bad Guy flew backward.

I pushed off the *Revenge* up near the airlock. The woman came with me. I kicked out and flipped. My legs threw the woman toward the far wall. She tried to resist, but my momentum flung her outward. She pulled me along, but lost her grip on my leg.

Roberre landed on his target outside the *Revenge*'s gravity field. The man grunted. Blood erupted from his mouth.

Earl caught his man's gun as he fell.

I windmilled my arms to right myself midair. I passed the gravity field margins and dropped. Angel's Planet brought me down. My feet hit first, banging my heels. My soles slipped. I landed on my butt.

The woman flipped midair, as good as I could have done. She landed in a crouch. She popped up and aimed her rifle at me.

Two shots rang out.

The woman dropped her rifle. She stared at the two holes in her chest a few centimeters apart. Then she swore and sank to the floor. Blood splattered all over.

Jackson groaned as he climbed his feet. "In your other pants?"

I shrugged. "*Revenge* off." Gravity returned to normal. The shimmer disappeared, but by then we were all outside the zero-g area anyway. It still felt like the last move in the strange kidnapping. We'd survived.

I rolled to my feet and rubbed my butt. I was going to be sore. I walked over and stared up into Earl's face. "Where did you learn to do that?"

He glanced down at the gun, puzzled. He seemed rather stunned that he'd just killed two people. "I...um...I do not know."

Jackson walked over and gently took the gun from Earl. "Earl Montague Cristo be at peace. Fear not. All is well."

Roberre trotted over, too, tracking blood. "Woof."

Earl laid a hand on Roberre's head and visibly relaxed; his face returned to its normal placid expression.

Then I noticed the man Roberre had landed on. His chest was crushed. How much did Roberre weigh?

Earl had accounted for all three of these murderers.

"Um...we should get out of here."

Jackson clasped my shoulder. "And get the data crystal from your other pants. That was well done."

Earl squatted to face Roberre's mechanical eyes. "I believe I will come with you. Roberre, let's get our stuff."

Earl rose, and together they walked off to the storeroom on the other side of the *Revenge*.

Jackson elbowed me. "Well, Kid, it looks like we're taking care of the bodies. I say we move them over by the wall opening and let them fall down the Precipice when we leave."

By the time we'd dragged five bodies over by the wall where the floor tilted down to let ships in and had retrieved said data crystal from my other pants, Earl emerged from his machine shop. Roberre followed, pulling a cart loaded with tools, a gravity field analyzer, a micro fusion pile, a hydrogen purifier, and other equipment piled high. Earl didn't even glance at us as he led Roberre up the ramp.

I wanted a shower, but it was time to fly so I followed Earl. "Come on, old man, let's get—"

Something crashed against the outer door.

3
RETURNING TO EXILE

I paused on the *Revenge*'s cargo ramp as someone tried to batter down Earl's outside door. Another crash was followed by an explosion.

As soon as Jackson and I were both on the ramp, I hit the button on my bracer to close it. I dashed up into the cargo hold.

In the mostly empty hold, Earl and Roberre secured the gravity cart that held his precious tools and equipment.

I made the one-eighty to reach the ladder against the *Revenge*'s rear wall beside the ramp, then I hollered at Earl. "Strap in and open the shop floor!"

I scrambled up the ladder. "*Revenge* on!"

The gravity drive came online by the time I reached the common room at the rear of the personnel deck, Jackson in tow. The room, which was used for many purposes, had an airlock aft and a corridor going forward.

I dashed down that corridor, past the head, galley, two bedrooms, and food storage to the bridge. Through the bulkhead door, the bridge's shielded-glass canopy opened before me, showing Earl's shop floor from above. Two reclining seats were recessed into the floor, each with a pair of joysticks.

I grabbed my helmet off the peg, put it on, and jumped into the left-hand seat. Then I jacked in, buckled my belts, and rushed the preflight checks. Virtual Vision erased the bulk of the *Revenge*, letting me see beyond the ship in any direction. It also gave me a heads up display of all relevant systems.

Jackson took the other seat.

I lifted the *Revenge* off the ground and rotated it.

The floor tilted downward, Earl's work. Five bodies fell down the tall cliff. The pressurized room kept most of Planeta de Angel's toxic atmosphere out.

I tipped the *Revenge*'s nose down and moved out, dead slow. As we emerged below the shop, a gust pushed us sideways.

Going where the air chose, I tipped the *Revenge* into the wind. We cleared the shop. I pushed the *Revenge* up higher. The Precipice spread below us. When I rose above the immediate vicinity of the spaceport, I hit a full four gs. The *Revenge* surged upward. Thermals from the lava flows tossed us around.

I still had some boost left in the jump capacitors from my approach to Angel's Planet. But I wouldn't use it unless I needed to.

At this point, I didn't even know where we should go. I glanced over at Jackson. "Will the Romans have any ships...?"

A blip appeared on my radar; a ship hidden in the clouds, not even in orbit. It wasn't descending or flying out either. I swore.

Jackson tilted his head. "I'm going to say yes."

The ship might be something benign, though I doubted it. I turned right, away from that ship, still rising. I angled for a giant volcanic ash plume.

For a little while, the other ship didn't move. Then it accelerated hard toward us and fired three missiles.

Lasers and plasma cannons didn't have the range in an atmosphere. He might have fired a railgun though. I jigged right and down. My proximity alarms went off. It saw the ash as solid. I disabled the automatic avoidance system.

"Can you take those missiles?"

"Depends how good your targeting computer is," Jackson said and turned on the weapons system.

The missiles closed in. I made the ash plume. Visible light vanished. I had gravity scan, which didn't work well near a planet, and radar. The volcanic heat lifted the *Revenge*.

Jackson fired the laser cannon. One missile vanished. The second got close and exploded. Shrapnel pinged off the hull. An alarm showed a hull breach in the common room. Bulkhead doors slammed shut.

Ash and methane could hurt the interior. And they'd damaged my ship!

"Boost!"

The power released from the capacitor back to the drives pushed the *Revenge* over four and a half gs. Acceleration pressed me back into the smart padding of the pilot's chair. My cheeks tried to touch my ears. My hands on the joysticks weighed a ton.

Eight missiles launched from the spaceport. At the enemy ship. Angel didn't like military ships near his planet.

The jump light came on.

I hit the button. The atmosphere of Angel's Planet stretched and faded. Ash came with us. *Hiram's Revenge* pushed through a gravitic point-anomaly into the pocket universe known as Lu Space. The weird, non-relativistic relationship between Lu Space and the regular universe let us cover about a light-year a day.

I hadn't aimed. Or set a course.

I powered the *Revenge* back to three gs and turned on the compensators, a move most ships couldn't do in Lu Space without blowing up their reactors. Weight came off my body. I vertical-shifted, rotating the *Revenge* to fly top first, so gravity was down toward the deck.

Jackson started to unbuckle. "Well, that was fun."

I grabbed his arm to stop him. "Wait. We aren't going far."

Had the destroyer survived? If so, it might have noted what direction I'd gone. I turned the *Revenge,* another maneuver most ships couldn't do yet. With all those maneuvers, more feedback added energy to the capacitor and my boost light came on.

I stayed in Lu Space for five minutes, which put us well beyond the solar system. Then I hit the fallout button. Gravity vanished and I floated into my straps. The strange colors behind the ash stretched and brightened. On a plume of light and heat, we re-entered normal space, far from any planet or star.

Ash from the volcano floated around us, which annoyed me. For a moment I let us drift. How could I get rid of the stuff? If I turned on my drives, all the ash would be sucked in closer. Any momentum I gave the *Revenge,* would also be imparted to the ash.

But gravity could be used to push as well as pull. I just didn't have the controls for it. Punching up a virtual keyboard, I started through my control subroutines.

Jackson stirred against his straps since we were all still weightless. "What are you doing?"

I shrugged. "Normal stuff that no one has ever thought of before."

Jackson tapped my helmet in time with his words. "Will you stop changing the rules?"

I snorted. "Not a chance. There are more things in heaven and Earth, Jackson, than are dreamt of in your philosophy."

It didn't take long since all I had to do was reverse one vector. I powered up the drives at zero g, then stomped the main thrust pedal. My hair tried to stand on end. My stomach tried to come out of my mouth, but some bile reached my throat instead. The ash flew away, scattered into deep space.

I let off the pedal. The strange outward gravity went away.

Then I saved the subroutine off to the side for possible later use and powered the drives back to a sedate one gravity.

"That was...interesting." Jackson folded his arms. "Can I get up now?"

I rolled my eyes, which he couldn't see. "No." I flipped on the intercom. "How are you doing down there, Earl?"

His inflectionless voice came back through the speakers. "The hull breach is repaired."

Well, he was back to normal, not to mention handy to have around.

I brought up the life support controls. "Thank you. Go back down to the cargo hold and seal the hatch. I want to clean the upper deck."

A few minutes later, I sucked all the air from the personnel deck, which let the quantum filters clean out all the ash. When I'd re-pressurized everything, I finally let Jackson up.

Together, we walked back to the common room. When Jackson turned and opened his mouth to speak, I shoved him. "What the hell did you get me involved in?" I shoved him again. "Seven people are dead! Earl and I can't go back to Angel's Planet!"

I'd have been gentler if he hadn't been grinning at me.

When Jackson's back reached the far wall, I shoved him anyway. "They tried to kill us! What is this about? Why the hell are *you* even here? You're retired!"

Jackson folded his arms. "Are you done?"

"No!" I pointed to the new patch in the port side wall. "You damaged my ship too!

Roberre, bounded up the ladder and sniffed at Jackson. "Woof."

I put my hands on my hips. "Exactly. Now explain."

With a big sigh, Jackson sat on the couch. "I'm sorry. That did not go as expected. I'm too old for this. I only got involved because someone thought I would be less threatening, and knew I was already on Planeta De Angel." He pulled the data crystal from his pocket. "This has information on Roman spy activities on Eksil since the Council of Planets ended the Roman blockade."

That quenched my anger or at least redirected it. I'd carried Eksil's ambassador, Mikka Retts, to Earth at considerable risk. In a lot of ways, she was the one that got me to end my exile. Or at least make a start at it.

I took the crystal from Jackson and held it up. If I set up an isolated virtual computer that I could connect a reader slot to and safely examine the crystal. We were supposed to take it to Thurman. We almost certainly didn't have authority to read whatever was on it.

I paced two steps to the other side of the room and back. "The Romans know we have this and that we escaped. By the time we go to the authorities, and they get back to Eksil, none of this will be useful."

Jackson turned a hand up. "The transfer didn't go so well."

Helping Mikka felt right to me. Usurping a spy operation with no backup and no authority was the height of hubris, if not outright stupidity. But Mikka had invited me, trusted me, even befriended me, and Eksil would have resources.

I cocked my head at Earl. "My friend, what say we go fight some Roman spies on Eksil?"

That fierce intensity returned to Earl's eyes. "Romans..."

Roberre nudged him and gave a little *wuff*.

Absently, Earl reached down to pat Roberre's head. His ordinary, placid expression returned.

An emotional support robot?

Earl nodded. "I would anticipate that with considerable relish."

I started for the bridge. "I'll set course and get us back to Lu Space."

Jackson chuckled. "Are you going to ask me?"

I walked backward a moment. "Of course not. You got us into this, and you're outvoted. You could cook us some supper."

An hour later, after I got us on course for Eksil, we sat down to a barbecued pork dinner with coleslaw and mustard sauce. Jackson apologized for not taking all day to cook it. I set up my little, isolated virtual computer, connected a socket, and put the data crystal in.

It took no time to find the one file. Understanding the database took a little longer, mostly because I expected codes or secrets or something.

At last, I saw what it meant and swiped the data up onto the wall. "It's a list of ships. Name, registry, home planet, and captain, plus some dates. That's all that's on here."

Jackson stopped with a bite of coleslaw halfway to his mouth. "You'll have some detective work to do when we get there."

I pointed at the back door. "Do you want me to throw you out the nearest airlock?"

Jackson smiled but smacked the little table. "You're the one who said my vote didn't count."

I stood and leaned against the wall next to the corridor, arms folded. "You're the one who conspired with the bastards who created me."

"Woof!" Roberre said.

I stared at the robot dog, mouth open. Then I broke up laughing.

When I recovered, I sat back down and took another bite of barbeque. I chewed and frowned, thinking. "Well, the government on Eksil will help. They like me, after all."

★★★★★

Two months later, I hit the fall-out button within range of Eksil for a standard approach, with Earl and Roberre below and Jackson in the copilot's seat. The strange colors in Lu Space stretched and brightened into a plume of light. When the light faded, the orange star was a tiny dot, and Eksil a blue and white orb. My scans found ships. As when I came to break the Roman blockade, there were gravity drive ships in orbit around the planet, though only a few now.

Even though I had been here before, the planet seemed so odd with the ice cap on the equator in the dark night. A ring of clouds and storms marked the twilight area and extended just into the dark side.

I shook my head. "Still can't believe these people live on a tidally locked planet."

Then my radar and gravity scan found something else, something big, that appeared to be in a polar orbit.

"What's that? A space station? How did they get a station here so fast?"

Jackson smacked my shoulder. "It's been over a year. I'm fairly sure that station is from the African Geological Expedition out of New Serengeti. They're fast."

That made sense. Akeem, one of my classmates at Solomon Tech, worked for AGE, and he was always thinking of new ways to move and build large stations.

I altered course to dock at the station. I flipped over, so gravity was still toward the deck. We decelerated in a sedate manner. As we neared, the station resolved on the telescope to a modest affair with four standard small-ship docks and ports for four shuttles.

Thirty minutes in, there was a flash and a second and a third, behind me. The ships were several light minutes out. When I magnified, though, I found three star sharks. Two CPN Destroyers left orbit and moved out toward the *Revenge*, but at a leisurely pace and without jumping. I watched, well behind reality. The sharks all floated inward for a minute, then turned and jumped back out again.

When the sharks left, the destroyers laid off thrust and drifted without hailing me.

I frowned, puzzled. "I think the star sharks just checked us out. But why?"

Jackson stirred in his seat. "They don't like coming in this far—this close to the sun—that I've ever seen. Perhaps they want to know what we're doing."

I took a long breath. This couldn't be the first time that happened. "The station will know more."

I opened a channel and got landing clearance. Two hours later, I set *Hiram's Revenge* down on the station platform. The docking tube connected to my rear airlock, and I shut down the drives. Then I let the vibrations drain from my body.

Jackson got up and headed back. By the time I had unbuckled, jacked out, gone to my room, and changed out of my flight suit into just a pale green shirt and charcoal pants, Earl had reached the common room. He equalized the air pressure so we could open the airlock doors.

A little later, the three of us walked out through the docking tube into the station proper. I paused at the way the air smelled. It reminded me of Mikka. Was it perfume? Native plants?

A woman bounced up with a big smile. She was short with a wide nose and tightly curled blonde hair, like a gold nimbus around her head. She also wore a pin like the one Mikka had me put on my fake uniform, except hers had a bronze triangle and two blue ones in a bronze circle. "Hej! Welcome to Eksil. My name is Airini. We're so glad you've kom. What is your business?"

What was my business? Catching spies? "I'm Deuce, and I need to talk to someone with authority."

For a moment, Airini just gaped. Then she threw her arms around me. "Oh! You fløj Rådmand Retts to Earth! Takker dig! Takker dig!" She broke away before I could even pat her back. "Oh! I must let everyone kende!"

That wouldn't do. Kende? Did she mean *know*? She shouldn't let *anyone* know. "Airini! I need my arrival to be quiet. You may know who I am and let one person with some authority know. That's all. No one else."

Airini came up short and turned back. Then she waved her arms to encompass the world. "But...alle sammen will want to takker dig!"

I walked over to her and laid a hand on her shoulder. "I understand. We can tell them later. For now, I have important business." I held up a finger. "*One* person with authority, and not in a public place."

"Oh, very well. This way, and we'll start your entrance exam while I finde someone for you to sige with."

She beckoned us on through the inner airlock door and into the station proper.

I glanced over my shoulder at Jackson. "Entrance exam? We have to take a *test* to get in?"

Jackson spread his hands, amused. "Not if you don't want to, Dear."

Rolling my eyes, I turned and followed Airini into the central core. To my bracer, I said, "*Revenge*, lock."

Behind us, the ship beeped to confirm the security system was active and there was an audible thunk as the physical lock slid home. We'd left Roberre as a guard, too.

On this level of the space station, there were nothing but airlock doors to more docking tubes and an elevator, though there was a colorful mural on the walls—painted, not digital— of an orange sun in an aquamarine sky. Airini held the elevator door for us.

Earl, Jackson, and I hurried on. The elevator was large, big enough for freight, but painted in calico colors. Airini took us up one level. The door opened on a wider ring, with the low hubbub of half a dozen people chatting.

We stepped out into an office on that occupied one side of this level of the station. A café occupied the other half. A man and woman stood talking by a reception counter with an old-style computer on it. Two men and a woman leaned against the wall by the café snacking on bread stacked with meat, cheese, and a garnish. All five of them had similar circular pins, with reds and blues dominant.

The three in the café saw us and put down their food. "Hej! Visitors!"

The man near the office straightened up and stepped toward us. "Sabra, you know they have to see us first."

Sabra bounced over to the deli counter and grabbed three cheese Danishes. "They can spise while you poke and prod, Varick!!"

Varick rolled his eyes, but he let Sabra give us the Danish. Then he opened the door behind him and gestured for us to enter.

Since it appeared we had to go through this to get down to the planet, I followed Varick in. The room beyond had colorful walls and archaic medical equipment, needles, vials, and the like. Smiling, Varick indicated a chair, so I sat.

He sat beside me and logged into a computer, also archaic. "First we need information, as in your name and the reason for your visit."

I started to say Deuce but realized here Deuce was famous and no one would know Burgundy Lee. It was a little like Brandy, the legendary star pilot, not wearing her trademark shades when I was born. No one recognized her out of disguise. I still had a photo of that encounter. Here, no one would know me as Burgundy either.

I smiled. "I'm Burgundy Lee, and I'm here to...see the sights."

He didn't bat an eye at that. Apparently, other tourists had come. Given my spectacular landing in the Forbidden City and the uproar Mikka and I had created in Beijing, everyone knew about Eksil now.

After that, Varick took my picture, drew my blood, and put the vial into the one modern piece of equipment there.

Varick tapped the thing with affection. "The nice people from AGE got us these DNA analyzers. Without them, it still takes us days to do this."

He hummed a little tune until the DNA analyzer chimed. Then he connected his computer to the analyzer with an old-style cable. He hummed some more, forming a strange harmony with the beast of a printer as it churned out an ID.

When it finished, Varick picked up the card without looking. "Sometimes I think someone is dreaming about these computers. Does anyone really know how they værk?"

Well, I did, but I didn't feel like expanding on that.

Varick glanced at the card with my name, picture, and a gold border as he held it out. "Oh! That's a first."

I took the card and held it up. "What is?"

"Um, well, we measure genetic potential. And this is the first gold we've had. There've been a couple silvers."

"Genetic potential?" I suddenly felt like I was being compared to Brandy again.

Varick shrugged. "Sure. When we got here, we had a tiny population, so we needed to get the best we could from everyone."

The woman drawing blood from Earl waved his gold-rimmed card. "Hey, Varick, this one's a gold!"

I rolled my eyes. "Try the old man. He's probably a purple or something."

That got Varick to laugh. "We only have the five levels, gold through red."

While Varick went to draw blood from Jackson, I ate my Danish, and the woman laid a hand on Earl's shoulder. She handed the card to him with a smile. "I get off in three hours, if you want someone to show you around."

Earl glanced at the woman, but did not offer so much as a grin. "That would be enjoyable, but I have other plans."

Varick finished drawing Jackson's blood, then Airini stuck her head in. "We have the destroyer *Lexington* ready for their R&R. Also, another trade ship is inbound." Then she turned to me. "I've arranged your meeting as requested. Would you like to flyve down or take the shuttle?"

"Thank you, Airini. We'll fly down."

I was not about to leave my ship up here where I had no control over who had access. I'd upgraded the security system, after the *Revenge* almost got stolen while on Earth with Ambassador Retts, but anything could be overcome with time. And I suspected the Roman spies would try for my ship again.

I rose as Varick's printer chugged to his hummed harmonies again, printing Jackson's card. It came out silver. Varick frowned a little as he held it up. "Well, that's disappointing. I was hoping for three in a row."

Airini led us back to the dock. "Just land at the spaceport in Nyhagen, such as it is. Someone will meet you."

I assumed Nyhagen would be the main city, since there only appeared to be one. The three of us boarded *Hiram's Revenge* and set out to find Roman spies.

4
MASTER OF GAMES

Twenty minutes later, we had received clearance and coordinates for the new spaceport. I lifted *Hiram's Revenge* gently off the station and headed southward toward that ocean next to the mountain range where I'd touched down to get Mikka. With the storm at the edge of the night whipping up the wind, I tipped the nose down and headed into the atmosphere.

Once I descended below the stratosphere, I let the winds take the *Revenge* where they would, toward the city. I enjoyed the wind on the *Revenge*'s control surfaces. It reminded me of the planes at Goldblum's Flying Circus back on New Zion when I was in college, and that reminded me of Hiram and what might have been if not for the bastards who'd created me.

It also reminded me of the first time I'd been here, screaming down through the atmosphere with my drives off, depending on air to hold the *Revenge* up. And of how befriending Mikka had shown me the loneliness of my exile.

Almost a year later, I still had no home.

Now, as the upper-level air currents that flowed toward the night side changed to dark-to-light winds lower down, the moisture precipitated out into storms. The *Revenge* shook even more. I smiled. And I did have friends—Jackson and Earl, oh boy.

The mountain range came into view, and the ocean beyond it. We descended, crossing the mountains and hitting a thermal over the water. It wasn't a big ocean, about the size of the Caspian Sea, though I'd been going a lot faster when I'd crossed the Caspian back on Earth on the way to Beijing when I'd taken Mikka there, since I'd had destroyers above and missiles on my tail.

At last, Nyhagen spread before us, as big as Pauley City. Well, as big as Pauley City before all the people immigrated from Earth. As we got closer, we found the spaceport, based on the coordinates. It had runways like an old-fashioned airport from the history books, with a big Tarmac added to the south. Also, sunward of the city, but not far, was another complex of some sort—a lot of buildings without a clear purpose I could see.

A fusion jet took off while we watched, heading toward the darkness on takeoff then turning south. Spaceport control gave me landing clearance. A few minutes after that, I set *Hiram's Revenge* down at the end of a row of ships on a newly poured tarmac. The other dozen ships were mostly small freighters of similar size to the *Revenge*, although there were two small passenger liners, the kind diplomats would use.

I shut down the *Revenge*, but paused before jacking out. I was always sad to land. It usually meant the adventure was over. Not this time, though.

I unbuckled, jacked out, and left my helmet on the seat when I rose. Then I walked out to the common room, Jackson in my wake. I grabbed an overnight bag from my quarters as I went by, since it was likely we wouldn't need to fly for a while. Jackson did the same. Since there wasn't a docking tube, I led Jackson down to the cargo deck. Earl and Roberre waited for us there.

I squatted by Roberre and patted his head. "Well, boy, do you think you can stay here and guard the ship?"

Roberre glanced up at Earl, then sat on his haunches. "Woof."

I rose and touched my bracer to lower the ramp. "Good. No one gets in here but us."

When the ramp got to the ground, Earl, Jackson, and I walked out. By then, a car was waiting, silver and blue with a logo on the front door that appeared derived from the Olympic rings.

I stopped on the tarmac, hands on hips. "It has wheels!"

Jackson shoved to get me going. "They don't have gravity drives. Stop gawking."

A driver emerged from the front and opened a rear door for us. As we approached, I noticed he had a blue pin with one bronze and two blue quadrants. We climbed in and found two forward-facing and two rear-facing seats, one occupied by a young woman with reddish hair. I ended up next to her. When my eyes adjusted, I saw she had a gold pin with three silver quadrants. What were these pins?

The woman beamed. "Hi! I'm Assistant Master of Games Vada Retts."

Retts? I did a double take. "Wait. Are you Mikka's daughter?"

Mikka couldn't have a daughter almost as old as me.

Vada leaned over and hugged me. "You're Deuce, right? I'm so glad to meet you. Mom has told me so much about you. We're all so grateful."

For a moment, her words flowed over me like Kaia's, and it felt so nice. When Vada, at last, released me, I raised a hand to stop the torrent. "You get to know something your mother does not. My real name, which is Burgundy. No one else should know I'm Deuce, at least for now."

For a moment, Vada gaped. Then she shook her head. "These intriger are all so fremmed to us. Why are they necessary?"

Had she said intrigues are foreign to us? I was about to shock her again, so I gestured toward the ships at the spaceport. "Well, if my quick count is right, I'd say half those ships on the Tarmac are working for the Romans."

"What? That can't be. We..." Vada's face darkened, and her nostrils flared in anger. She spoke through clenched teeth. "Which ones?"

At least she caught on quickly.

I held up a finger. "First, before we arrest them or kick them off the planet, we need to find out why they are here. Second, it may be useful to not let them know you know."

Vada closed her eyes and nodded. "That's why you didn't want to meet the Råd. It would be known that you did. I see. It is why they sent me, my house will be quiet and unobserved. I can relay what you need to them. What do we need to do?"

The driver started the car, then turned and drove off the tarmac. I felt every uneven spot in the road. I put my hands on the seat beside me and watched out the window. How did people put up with such a bumpy ride?

Jackson laughed. "You'll have to pardon her. She's not used to wheels or touching the ground at all."

I kicked him, then turned back to Vada. "We will need to inform the Råd, whatever that is, and find out what these spy ships have traded for. They want something here, but we don't know what." I pointed toward the sky. "Wait, on the station, they called your mom a Rådmand. What is that?"

Vada blinked and her mouth fell open. "Oh! There are so mange tings we take for givet. The Råd is our ruling, um, council. And a Rådmand is a councilor. There are seven, although with my mom away on Earth, there are only six until the next games."

Now it was my turn to stare, open mouthed. Now some of what Mikka said or assumed made sense. "You choose your rulers with games?"

"Of course. How do *you* choose your rulers?" She pointed at me.

I glanced out the window. We weren't heading into the city but sunward toward that complex I'd seen from above. "Um, lots of ways. Mostly by voting, these days."

Vada furrowed her brow. "But how do you make sure the most qualified people get the jobs?"

I resisted smiling at Vada. This sounded so much like my conversations with Mikka. "Uh, well, we don't."

Maybe if we had, the bastards who made me wouldn't have been in power. Although, at this point, I wanted to exist. I would just rather the bastards didn't.

Vada pouted. "That sounds inefficient, perhaps dangerous."

We approached a group of three houses close to the game complex, and the driver pulled up by one about the size Cinti's, the woman who'd flown with my sister and helped me buy the *Revenge*, except this one was painted more like a calico cat with reds and oranges and whites.

When the car stopped, three children burst from the front door. A girl about five or six, and two boys, both younger. The youngest, around three, toddled behind. The girl had chestnut hair, the older boy tight black curls, and the toddler was a pale blond. Kaia's kids appeared similar, like they belonged together. These could have come from separate families.

An older woman appeared at the door, hands on hips and exasperated. I knew that expression from Kaia. The memory made me smile.

Vada opened the door on her side and popped out to greet them. I followed, shouldering my bag. All three kids piled into Vada for a big family hug. She tousled the toddler's hair, then turned them all toward us. "Kids, these are our new venner, Burgundy, and...Oh, dear!" She put her hand to her mouth as she realized she hadn't introduced herself to either Earl or Jackson.

I took over, indicating each of my associates. "This big lunk is Earl, and the old man is Jackson."

Embarrassed and blushing, Vada laid a hand on her daughter's shoulder. "This scamp is Tamara. My little man is Dural, and my baby here is Damien."

Damien pouted and stomped his foot. "Not a baby!"

Living with Kaia had given me some kid-experience. I squatted in front of Damien. "Of course not. And what would a big boy like you want to do?"

He pointed back toward the house, or past it. "Games. Gamila won't let us."

Vada smiled. "We'll go after we eat. Our new venner have never been to the game complex."

Dural's mouth fell open, but he turned to his mom. "How not?"

Tamara's eyes grew wide. "Never?" She turned to us, quite serious. "Then you *must* go, I will show you around."

Vada herded them back toward the house. "Everyone, go wash up."

I rose and smiled at Vada. "You have a nice family."

"Takker dig!" She headed in. "Now, about those Roman spioner. What do we do?"

The three of us followed up the steps and inside. The foyer had murals of sports and games. It opened into an airy living room that had several soft chairs and skylights overhead. The sunward side of the house, directly across from the foyer, had a hallway going back with open doors on each side, but no windows at all. A stairway on the living room's left led to a second floor that appeared to be a big, open balcony over the foyer.

Gamila herded the kids off to the right, into a kitchen with bright tiles.

I stopped and put my hands on my hips. "Well, first it would be good if we could find out what the spies have purchased." I pulled the printout from my pocket. "From what I can tell, most of these are traders of some kind or other."

Taking the sheet, Vada read the simple list. She shook her head. "I wouldn't know. However, I will get this list to Rådmand Balbuk, who's in charge of commerce."

I gave her a nod. "That's a start. We'll need—"

My bracer beeped.

An intruder trying to get into the *Revenge*!

Earl stared into the distance. "Roberre has detected an intruder hacking the airlock door."

I whirled on Vada. "We need your driver to take us back. Now!"

Jackson shooed Earl and me away. "You two rescue the ship. I'll go to the game complex with Vada."

With my bag bouncing on my shoulder, I dashed toward the door. I paused to glance over my shoulder. "Send whatever police you have to the port."

The driver was about to leave but stopped when he saw me. "Take us back to the port. Hurry!"

5
Hijacked

Earl and I sat in the back of the car as we bumped along the roads, much faster than when we'd come. I willed the driver to go faster still while I fidgeted. The Romans would not take the *Revenge*. I wouldn't allow it.

Then I remembered my upgrades and tapped a button on my bracer. "*Revenge*, virtual lock."

My bracer beeped, signaling the gravity drives were offline and the software to access them locked down, too. Then it created virtual control software, linked to the joysticks, but not the ship, so it wouldn't control anything.

As the driver careened back down the roads we'd driven much more sedately before, I fished in my bag for my plasma pistol, holster and all. When I found it, I considered strapping it to my waist. Instead, I tossed it to Earl.

He caught it in one hand. Then he unholstered it, flipped it and powered it on. The fierceness had returned to his eyes. He held the pistol loosely, like an extension of his arm, but did not point it at me even once.

Firing that pistol on board the *Revenge* would burn holes, so I reached slowly across and turned the power down three notches. It would still kill but would not blast through the walls.

When we got to the space port, I leaned over to see if I could see anything amiss, but the *Revenge* appeared normal, all the doors closed. The intruders must have overridden the electronic locks on the main airlock. Difficult, but not impossible. Perhaps I needed better locks.

I raised the bracer. "*Revenge,* lower ramp. Open airlock doors."

The driver swung the car around the line of ships, rear end fishtailing out. He screeched to a stop behind the *Revenge.*

Earl leapt from the car ahead of me. He dove onto the ramp before it was halfway down and crawled up. I grabbed a jacket from my bag. Then I clambered from the car and dashed over. At the *Revenge,* I hustled up the outside ladder to just below the airlock door.

I swung the jacket across the opening.

A shot rang out.

It tore my jacket from my hand. Roberre's "woof" came from inside. Then a crunch. Someone cried out. My plasma pistol fired.

A pair of cars screeched up behind me. Two men and two women piled out. They did not seem to be armed. One pointed up at me. "What are you doing up there?"

Earl called from inside. "All clear."

"Woof!"

I held on with one hand and turned to what I hoped were police officers. "Hello, officers. I am trying to rescue my ship."

A short man with tight black hair put hands on hips. "How do we know this is your ship?"

I pointed at Vada's driver. "Ask him."

Given their reaction, not to mention Earl's, if he showed up in the airlock door holding a plasma pistol while in meaning mode, it would not be good.

I stuck my head up over the threshold. "Earl, the police are here. What's the situation?"

"Woof!" said Roberre.

Earl stepped into the airlock; hands empty, but eyes flashing. One hand lay on Roberre's head, and he relaxed as we all watched. "One intruder is dead, Captain. The other is ready for interrogation."

"Good. Well done."

I started down the ladder.

What was up with Earl? It seemed Roberre had not been able to bring him back quite as quickly.

The short officer, though still taller than me by half a head, seemed to be in charge. He stepped up to me when I reached the ground. "I am Detective Bossen. May I see your ID card, please?"

I produced the gold-rimmed thing, which reminded me of Brandy, again.

Bossen got out a device I didn't recognize and scanned the card. It beeped, and he checked the results. "Hmm. We will need to verify this." He indicated the ramp. "Let us go see what has happened here."

I led the four of them up the ramp, then turned right to the ladder at the rear of the ship. When we emerged in the common room, we found two intruders. One had a plasma burn through his chest. The other one moaned in a pool of blood in the corridor to the bridge. He had two broken legs. I guessed he'd run into Roberre. Both had firearms nearby. My plasma pistol was on the table in the common room.

Earl, with his hand still on Roberre's head, stood in the airlock, facing in now. His expression and his eyes had returned to their normal bland calm.

Bossen inspected the scene. "So it's your conjecture that these two broke into your ship to steal it." He pointed at Earl. "And that this man killed one and incapacitated the other using that weapon." He pointed to the pistol on the table.

I nodded. "Yes, sir. After one of them fired at *me*. You will find my coat, with a big hole in it, on the ground outside."

The officer frowned at the whole scene. "Offworlders." Then he clicked the microphone on his lapel. "Send an ambulance and crime scene investigators to the spaceport immediately."

At last, Bossen gestured toward the ladder down to the cargo deck. "If you will accompany me to the station, we'll continue this investigation."

I pursed my lips and shook my head. "I'm sorry, sir, I can't do that. Not until everyone is off my ship and I've locked it up again. I would also request guards outside here for the time being."

After an impressive glare, Bossen nodded once and indicated a chair by the table. Then he had one of his men bag my plasma pistol and move it elsewhere.

I sat down and gestured for Earl to take the other chair.

And there we waited.

The EMTs came and took broken-legs away. The crime scene people came and checked everything—blood spatter, fingerprints, footprints, and more. They even took more blood from me and Earl. Roberre, who sat on his haunches right beside Earl, drew many wary glances.

Two hours later, I yawned. When was this day going to end? It was still light...Oh. It was always light outside. I yawned again.

Earl glanced at me. "Captain, you need sleep. Go. I will watch."

When had he started calling me captain? Didn't he need sleep, too?

I got up, which attracted the attention of all six people in the room, so I pointed down the hall. "I'm going to sleep."

Bossen scowled but didn't say anything. I threaded my way between the people and tiptoed around the evidence. When I got to my quarters, I shut the door, turned out the light and collapsed on my bunk in the pitch black. I didn't bother getting undressed.

It seemed like thirty seconds later someone knocked on my door.

I struggled out of a dream where faceless toga-wearing strangers shot at my coat. Sometimes with me in it, sometimes not.

"Lights!"

The lights came on in my quarters. No one was inside. The bed still had the acceleration netting over it, the built-in dresser and wardrobe hadn't been torn out. Good.

The knock came again. "Captain, they need you out here."

I stretched, swung my legs out of bed, and got up. With a little shake, I stepped over and opened the door. Earl stood in the corridor, face drooping with weariness.

I put my hands on my hips. "Time for you to sleep. Go!"

"Yes, Captain." He headed back toward the common room.

I followed. Two men sat in the two chairs. One was Detective Bossen. The other was dressed like a medic, but his pin had a gold setting with silver, bronze, and gold triangles. From what I'd seen, though it was a bit of a guess, that was not the pin of a medic or EMT. A doctor seemed more likely.

The doctor had black hair, a wide nose, and silver eyes.

While the officer glared, this new man smiled, eyes twinkling.

I almost came to attention. "Officer, have you concluded the investigation?"

Bossen stood. "We have verified that this is indeed your ship. However, we frown on people, especially visitors, taking their own action in criminal cases. It is reckless and dangerous. In this case, the criminals themselves were..."

As he struggled for exact words, the doctor grinned. "Reckless and dangerous?"

I struggled not to laugh.

The officer whirled on the doctor, then slowly brought his gaze back to me. "Yes, reckless and dangerous. We identified the men, from two different trade ships. Both starship engineers, apparently. The surviving one will not talk and is demanding he be givet back to his ship. What do you think?"

There was wanting revenge and punishment versus wanting to stop whatever else the Romans were doing. What did I want to do?

I considered the bridge, then faced the officer. "I want to move my ship over by the assistant game master's house. The *Revenge* is perhaps the most valuable ship in human space right now. I'd like to keep it."

The officer spread his hands. "And the prisoner?"

I shrugged. "Fit punishment. And ban the ships they both came from. Force them to return any merchandise they traded for, too."

The doctor stood and laid a hand on the officer's shoulder. "Detective, I believe you can handle the criminal. I will deal with the ship he came from. Takker dig."

The officer nodded once. "Yes, sir."

Not a doctor, then. But who?

As the officer started down the ladder to the cargo deck, the not-doctor called after him. "Make sure my, um, driver, stays." He gave me a wink then put hands on hips, a smile playing on his lips. "You, Captain Lee, do know how to make an entrance."

Who would come see me, who knew, or at least guessed, that I was Deuce? The list was small. Who was it that Vada had mentioned she would talk to about the list of ships and what they had purchased? They both knew I wanted secrecy.

I smiled. "Well, Rådmand Balbuk, if you just change the definition of possible, making an entrance isn't hard. You can call me Burgundy."

I liked people calling me by my real name. I would have to send word to Mikka on Earth.

Balbuk, puffed himself up and laid hand on chest. "You may call me sir." Then he deflated, sat, and leaned back. "Or Rasmus, whichever suits." He indicated the other chair.

Somehow, his lack of formality made me feel ornery. How far could I go? What would he let me get away with? Smiling, I sat next to one of Eksil's rulers. "How about Razzy?"

He folded his arms and cocked his head. "I hørt you were daring. Daring enough to catch these spioner? Um, spies?"

I liked Razzy. I assumed he was competent, too, so I could get behind him being head of a government.

"I am. I am not, however, a spy." I raised a finger. "First, what are the merchant ships buying?"

"Ah!" He pulled a computer from his pocket. "That I came prepared for."

He used his thumb to unlock the computer then tilted it so I could see. I'd rather expected him to swipe it up to the wall. These people needed to get up to modern compatibility standards.

I leaned in close to read the list for each ship, feeling the warmth of Razzy's arm.

The traders had purchased a lot of things that made sense: artwork, stories, jewelry, some with stones I didn't recognize, and other cultural items. Eksil did not have tech anyone in the Council of Planets would want.

I was about to ask for clarifications on some of the items when Detective Bossen popped his head back up the ladder. "Captain Lee, you are needed. Game Master Vada tog your friend Jackson to the game complex. My men are on it, but when Vada and her children were ready to leave, he could not be found."

6
SEARCH

Jackson missing? Had the Romans kidnapped him?

After a stunned moment beside Razzy in the *Revenge*'s common room, I leaped to my feet and started for the bridge then stopped. "Detective Bossen, do I have permission to move my ship?"

He nodded once. "You do." He dropped back down the ladder.

Standing just into the short corridor to the bridge, I cocked my head at Razzy. "Rådmand, have you ever ridden in a gravity drive ship?"

Razzy chuckled. "*Now* you use my title. I've been up to the station a couple times."

My smile grew to an anticipatory grin. "Not on the bridge, then. Come on."

I beckoned him down the corridor, then hit the buttons on my bracer to close the ramp and the airlock.

Razzy gawked at the tiny galley and head, then whistled when we reached the bridge.

I handed him the spare helmet, took mine off Hiram's seat, and showed Razzy how to buckle up and jack the helmet in.

Not sure if the spies had done anything to the *Revenge* before I got there, I powered on the Virtual Vision then took the time to go through the pre-flight checks. I hesitated, before I started the drives. What could those spies have done?

I opened the intercom. "Earl! Wake up!"

I heard a muffled woof from Roberre. Then Earl said, "Yes, Captain?"

After I did deeper checks, I brought up the security videos. "Were those spies in here long enough to sabotage us?"

Earl grunted. "I will check."

The video showed the two men come into the airlock and make a beeline straight to the bridge. Roberre climbed the ladder from the cargo deck behind them. Then the robot dog went into Jackson's room.

The intruders spent a lot of time on the bridge. Then one of them came out and went into the galley. Was he getting *food*? That made no sense.

Razzy stirred in his seat and pointed at where the galley would be in his Virtual Vision. "He left something in the little kitchen."

"What?"

I replayed the recording. Sure enough, he was fingering something in his pocket, something rather bulky. When he came out, the bulk was gone.

About that time, the other one came out of the bridge, and the two of them chatted. Then I showed up and waved my coat by the back door.

The kitchen-spy stepped forward and shot my coat. Roberre charged out and ran into the bridge-spy. Earl popped up and used the double distraction to shoot kitchen-spy.

I flipped the mike open again. "Earl, check the galley."

While Earl investigated, I went through the thorough pre-flight list again. Then I went through the software and found that bridge-spy had gotten into my fake control software and tried to remove my voice-security.

Moments later, Earl popped into the bridge, though he was behind me where I couldn't really see him. "Captain, it appears they placed a toxic gas bomb in the stove exhaust such that you would spread the gas whenever you took off."

They wanted to discredit me? Make the people of Eksil think I wasn't trustworthy?

I waved toward the back. "Secure and preserve that for the police then strap in. And thank you."

Razzy pointed back over his shoulder. "That was subtle. We need to take care with these people."

The man had a point. All my security precautions couldn't prevent this sabotage. I wanted to turn Earl and Roberre loose on them.

I growled. "Yes."

While we waited, I powered on the drives, keeping gravity neutral. It did not take long for Earl to call back and say he was ready.

I lifted the *Revenge* off the ground, slowly, to a hundred meters. Then I punched the main thrust, hitting four gs straight up. I tipped the nose down and did a slow turn to locate the game complex.

I flipped the thrust out behind us. The *Revenge* shot down at an angle, nose first, but only at two gs. We weren't high enough for break-neck speed. I did a barrel roll, just because I hadn't gotten Razzy to yelp.

He still didn't.

As we approached the ground and Vada's house, I pushed the *Revenge* up over backward. Then I dropped the last ten meters.

Razzy cried out.

I powered down the *Revenge* and jacked out. "Now, isn't that better than riding in the back of a shuttle? Faster too."

Razzy sighed as he removed his helm. "Sure. Is daring related to reckless?"

I rose and offered him a hand up, his palm warm against mine. "First cousins."

I didn't wait for him then, I needed to find Jackson. Using my bracer, I opened the ramp. At the top of the ladder to the cargo deck, I stopped. What had Jackson done to get their attention? What did they want with him? Did they think he knew what I'd done to my ship?

I put my hands on my hips as Razzy made it into the common room. "Earl!"

He stuck his head out of Jackson's quarters, tall enough to see me over Razzy's head. "Yes, Captain?"

I scowled. "How do we find Jackson? Assume the Romans have him."

As if the word *Roman* opened a door, the fierce anger returned to his eyes. "We assume competence on his captor's part. Will the local police have the area he was taken covered? Checking witnesses and the like?"

Razzy turned to consider Earl, then nodded. "Yes, they will. This is a little outside their normal event, but they know how to block exits and talk to anyone who saw anything. Not to mention checking the security cameras."

"Come on." I went down the ladder, then turned and headed down the ramp. I wished I had my plasma pistol. I wanted to run.

"We need to see if Jackson left us a clue to his plans," Earl said, his voice sharp and intense behind me.

I barreled down the last meter of the ramp wanting to hit someone. A few meters away from *Hiram's Revenge*, I stopped. A police car sat in front of Vada's house. Down the hill at the game complex a dozen more waited, and officers seemed to be everywhere, swarming the complex and everyone near it.

They had that part in hand. I would be in the way down there. Razzy was correct about them, but did they know how to find Roman spies? Did I know any better?

With a growl, I strode toward the house instead. Earl and Razzy tried to keep up.

I brought my bracer up. "*Revenge*, close and lock."

When I reached the door, I hesitated and noticed the geometric designs carved into the wood. Rather than examine the artwork, I knocked, opened the door, and walked in.

"Hello?" My voice echoed in the foyer.

Gamila poked her head out from the kitchen. "Hej, Burgundy." She smiled, then her face fell. "Oh, Mr. Jackson is missing. He's not with you?"

I shook my head and led Razzy and Earl on into the living room with its stair and hallway out back. "No, he's not with us. Did he sleep here before he went to the game complex?"

"Ja." She indicated the back hallway. The dark one.

I gestured for her to precede me. "Show me."

Just as the four of us entered the twilight corridor, Vada emerged from one of the rooms and closed the door very softly. I recognized that move; a mother trying not to wake a child.

Barefoot, Vada walked silently toward us. "I'm so sorry. I feel like I failed you." She reached out a hand to me.

I leaned close. "Where is Jackson's luggage?"

Vada pointed at the door right beside us. "There. Why?"

Without waiting for an answer, she stepped through the door and waved a hand by the wall. A dim light came on.

I followed her in while Razzy, Earl, and Gamila stayed in the hall. The small room had a bed, a dresser, and most especially no windows. It even had dark gray walls.

Jackson's bag lay on the bed, with some clothes laid out on the dresser along with toiletries. Not sure what to do, I went over to paw through his bag. It felt like I was violating the privacy of my commanding officer. Or was he a friend? I really didn't know. He was just always there.

Then I found his computer pad underneath some underwear. He should have had it in his pocket. No one left their personal pad behind. Ever.

We could have used the computer to locate him, too. Except the Romans would have known that and taken it. Dread filled me. Its presence meant he'd known he would be kidnapped.

I picked up the little machine. It beeped and a video message popped up, as if it had been expecting me.

Jackson gave me a wink. "Hey, Burgundy. When you and Earl left, I realized I would be alone at the game complex. If you're seeing this, I was right. I expect the Romans think I know what you did to your ship. They will be disappointed. Broadcast on the Thurman beacon and you'll get a locator ping in response."

He reached up to stop the recording, then paused. "Oh, look up Samantha Kastanje."

The computer screen went blank. I just stared at it. Samantha Kastanje? Who could that be?

Only one person. My heart thumped in my chest. Oh, my.

7
SAM

Stunned, I stood like a statue in Jackson's dark little room in Vada's house. Vada unpiled Jackson's clothes on the dresser, even shaking them out.

Razzy stepped up to peer over my shoulder, a frown of concentration on his face. "Samantha Kastanje sounds familiar, like I should know who that is."

Vada rolled her eyes and gave him a playful shove. "You should. It's on the game master's test. Oldest person to win their first gold. She got silver at fifty-two, her first time to the main games, and gold at fifty-six. Then two more after that."

I stared up at the ceiling, not sure whether to curse Jackson or thank him. "Of course she did. As a pilot?"

Vada's eyes narrowed. "Yes, fusion VTOL jets. How did you know that?"

I knew who Samantha Kastanje really was, my sister, but the real story wasn't mine to tell, or not mine alone.

Taking Jackson's computer, I walked out of the room. "Just a guess."

Gamila and Earl seemed puzzled as Razzy and Vada followed me into the dark corridor.

I turned to walk backwards. "If you can find where this Samantha lives, I will go see her. On the way up, I will send the beacon broadcast Jackson suggested."

Vada shrugged. "I can find her. Why do you want to see her?"

Razzy didn't say anything, but his eyes narrowed, and he put a hand on Vada's shoulder to forestall her.

I didn't want him to touch her. I wanted him to touch me.

Where did *that* come from?

Gamila and Earl stayed in the background, like dutiful servants. That didn't seem right either.

I stepped over next to Razzy and put a finger on my lips. "If you could temporarily close the port, no ships in or out, and alert the destroyers in orbit, that would be helpful."

While Gamila went back to the kitchen, Vada, a little subdued, led Earl, Razzy, and me upstairs to her office. It had bright windows overlooking the game complex, paintings of athletes adorned the walls, and a desk that held one of those rather archaic computers like I'd seen up on the station.

Vada sat in the desk chair and got on her computer. I leaned over her shoulder, hoping she found Samantha and hoping she didn't. Vada connected to the games database— that's what the title on the screen called it. Then she opened the archives. When she typed in the name, it took the computer maybe twenty seconds to find it.

Vada followed the lines of data with her finger. "She chose to be a twilight bush pilot, flyvende miners and explorers in and out of the mountains and the twilight. She lives...um...in a place called Alice Junction just on the other side of the mountains."

She waved out toward the ocean, so I assumed she meant the mountains on the far side.

I straightened up and folded my arms. "Show me a map, not to Alice Junction—to her house."

Vada brought up a map and zoomed in on the mountains, then on a little town on a plain near a river on the far side. She found a house outside that village beside a stream. It had a hangar out back with a dirt runway. The place gave me déjà vu for Cinti and Joyce's house, and the hangar there, except this was smaller and simpler.

Jackson would need me, maybe us, soon, so I dashed back down the stairs, Razzy and Earl chased after me, much slower, and Vada struggled to keep up. Just as we reached the foyer, Detective Bossen stepped in through the front door.

He went immediately to Razzy at the foot of the stairs and came to attention. "Sir. Our initial search indicates Mr. Jackson left with a woman, arm in arm. He may have been drunk or drugged. We're tracking where they went when they left the game complex."

We could search for Jackson from both ends, so Bossen didn't really need to know about Jackson's instructions. Besides, the little house outside Alice Junction was private.

I whirled to face the stairs. Earl stood two steps up with Vada one step behind him. She gave Earl an appraising glance. She couldn't have him either. I brought him.

Wait. Where did *that* come from? Earl? Earl and me? Sometimes, I hated emotions like that.

I couldn't take Earl with me to meet Sam, so he needed a task. I gestured at the detective. "Earl, go with Detective Bossen. Help him interrogate any Roman spies they find."

The fierceness returned to Earl's eyes again. "Yes, Captain."

Whatever the Romans had done to this man was buried deep, and I guessed on purpose. Was I right to bring it back? Right now, though, he was the best weapon we had against them.

I laid a hand on Detective Bossen's shoulder and leaned in close. "Take a little care. His methods may not be gentle."

Bossen's eyes narrowed. He muttered, "We just don't know enough about this stuff."

I slapped him on the back. "I suspect you will learn fast."

He *would* learn fast, now that Eksil had been found by the outside world. There was something about the game complex and what Mikka had told me, but I didn't have time for that now. I had to find Samantha and Jackson.

I strode out of Vada's house. Razzy followed.

I turned and walked backward. "Rådmand, I need to do this one alone. Sorry."

With a smile, he touched his forehead. "Then I will keep track of Earl and the investigation from this end."

I wanted to give him a silly grin, or kiss him, but meeting my sister weighed on me. Turning, I dashed to my ship. "*Revenge* on, open airlock."

This time I clambered up the outside ladder and into the airlock. When I hit the common room, I told the *Revenge* to close it up.

Roberre emerged from Jackson's quarters. "Woof?"

I patted his head. "Earl had to stay behind. I'm afraid I'm using him. I hope it doesn't turn out badly."

"Woof." How did Roberre make that sound sad?

I walked to the bridge, sat down, donned the helmet, jacked in, and strapped in.

Soon, I lifted off at a reasonable pace, conflicted about this entire venture. Not only had I deprived Earl of his emotional support robot, but I was also about to disrupt Samantha's life in a very serious way. Jackson was gone and needed to be rescued. The Romans needed to be stopped, and Samantha could help with both. She would want to help with both.

Vada's house fell away, and the game complex, almost a small city to itself, spread below me, followed by the city. I turned the Revenge toward the ocean on the other side of the city as I gained altitude. I wondered how high I would need to be to use Jackson's locator.

I flew back northward over the ocean. When I reached ten thousand meters, I set my radio to broadcast to the Thurman planetary beacon—the frequency I would have used to ping Memnon station, if I had still been near Thurman, that is. I got a radio reflection on the same frequency, from someplace in the mountains.

Since I was flying that direction anyway, I sped up, crossing ocean and mountain. When the plains on the far side came into view, I repeated the broadcast. The second reply let me triangulate the position. Jackson was in the mountains. How had they gotten him that far in just a few hours? It meant a plane or spaceship of some kind.

I radioed back to the spaceport and had them relay the location to Detective Bossen.

Then I began my descent into Alice Junction. Thinking better of it, I detoured into the twilight. That way my approach wouldn't be quite so visible.

I ended up in a mild storm, so I extended my control surfaces and coasted down on the breeze.

I brought *Hiram's Revenge* in low, crossing a hundred meters before clearing the last of the tree-like plants. I landed beside the driveway in front of the house. With the *Revenge*'s aft end facing the house and hangar, I shut down.

I removed my helmet and unstrapped, then considered how to make my appearance. I decided for the dramatic since I wanted to be facing Samantha when she saw me. Down the ladder to the cargo deck I went. Then I walked out onto the ramp and used my bracer to lower it.

A chill wind with the smell of rain whipped into the ship while I descended. The house and hangar seemed to be made of wood and brick. Did they not have any big printers over here? Perhaps they didn't in such a small settlement. I had seen a road going west around the mountains toward Nyhagen.

Two pairs of boots appeared, followed by pants. Did someone else live here? I hadn't considered that. I was glad she'd found someone at last, but I was about to blow her cover, possibly blow up her life.

When the ramp reached the bottom, the woman from my baby picture faced me, but with more lines on her face and hair entirely white. It was still the face I saw in the mirror. The man next to her was a head taller than her, with steel-gray hair, a rugged face, and calloused hands.

When she saw me, Samantha, or Brandy, for it was surely her, took a deep breath and closed her eyes.

She reached out a hand and laid it on the man's arm. "I'm so sorry, dear."

I stepped off the ramp but didn't go closer.

The man glanced from Samantha to me and back. "I don't understand. Sorry for what? She does kind of look like you."

A sad smile grew on Samantha's face and a tear fell onto her cheek. "Oh, Taft, you are about to find out my deep, dark secret. I should have told you. I just couldn't bring myself to do it."

He smiled and bent down to kiss her forehead. "What? You think I didn't know you had secrets? You appeared out of nowhere at fifty-two to win a silver medal flyvende those jets. I am not worried you will leave me."

"Me? Leave *you*?" She put a hand on his neck and pulled him into a kiss.

It lasted long enough to get uncomfortable, but I kept my mouth shut, hands clasped behind my back. I examined the vegetation over by the river and took in the storms in the twilight. I wondered if the smell of rain meant the storm would reach here, too.

At last Samantha let him go, took his hand, and brought him over to me. "Taft, this is my sister Burgundy. And please call me Sam."

Taft raised an eyebrow. "Sister? I was going to guess granddaughter."

I'd read that biography about Brandy all those years ago. Was it right about how lonely she had been? Very likely. And asking me to call her Sam told me a great deal. Brandy was not here anymore.

I held out my hand. "Pleased to meet you, Taft. I think you have done for my sister what no one else has. That's important."

Taft shook my hand and leaned close to whisper. "I still don't know what she sees in me."

Sam leaned into Taft's shoulder. "I'm the lucky one...wait. You have a black ship, with atmospheric control surfaces." She pointed at the *Revenge* then wagged her finger first at herself, then me. "I'm ace. You're Deuce, aren't you? I should have known."

Taft put his hands on his hips. "If I'd known you had a sister, Old Woman, *I* might have guessed."

A slow smile grew on my face. "Yes, I took Rådmand Retts to Earth."

Sam waved at the sky. "It was *so* frustrating being down here with the Romans up there. I've never felt so impotent."

After what she'd done to the Romans in the war, it made sense she'd want to go kick their butts by herself. Unlikely she'd have succeeded, but telling Brandeis Clark she couldn't do something was a bad idea.

Not sure exactly what to do next, I just waited. The silence got a little awkward.

Sam touched Taft's arm, then stepped over and hugged me. The warmth and the acceptance seeped into my soul. I put my arms around her, and she whispered in my ear. "I'm glad you came. I've been dreading it and hoping for it." She pulled back, a little, holding both my shoulders. "When did Jackson tell you?"

Worry for Jackson settled like a stone in my stomach. I cocked my head and half smiled. "An hour ago, maybe two."

Sam's eyes flashed as she put hands on hips. "That old reprobate is *here*?"

I pointed with a thumb back toward Nyhagen. "Um, well, yes. We came to stop the Romans again. Now their spies have kidnapped Jackson."

Taft planted himself, tall and menacing. "More Romans? We've had enough of them!"

Sam grinned fondly at Taft, then stepped back. "Wait! What Roman spies? And why the hell would they kidnap Jackson?"

I ran a hand through my hair. "Well, maybe two-thirds of the merchant ships that put in here were spies or contracted by the Romans."

Sam folded her arms and tapped a foot. "Why do they want Jackson, exactly?"

I gestured back at *Hiram's Revenge*. "They think he knows what I did to my ship so I could break the blockade."

Sam pointed at the ramp. "You need my help? Let's get going."

I hesitated. My sister had flown fighters and destroyers, and all I had was a cargo ship. Still, I wanted to show her what *Hiram's Revenge* could do.

Taft stepped over and took Sam's hand. "May I kom?"

Sam cocked her head and winked at me. "He just wants to get into space."

Without waiting for an answer, Taft strode up the ramp. "Of course. Why else would I want to go?"

The three of us trooped up into my ship, with me sweating what my legendary sister would say about it. At the top of the ramp, Sam put her hands on her hips and inspected my cargo hold, mostly Earl's equipment.

She waved at it. "What's all this?"

About to point out the ladder on the right, I stopped. "That's the equipment my starship mechanic brought along. Because of Jackson, we had to make a rather hasty exit from Planeta De Angel, and I don't think any of us will be welcome back."

I stepped over and, with a flourish, indicated the ladder. "Honored guests, the living quarters are this way."

Taft snorted. "What menner du? I'm not honored nothing."

Sam led the way up the ladder.

Roberre growled. "Woof!"

I'd forgotten about Roberre!

I scrambled past Taft. "Roberre! Down, boy!"

Up in the common room, Sam stood frozen, hands raised. Roberre had her backed up against the wall. Roberre growled again.

I'd never had to do this before. Would Roberre listen to me? Or only Earl?

I reached up and laid a hand on Roberre's head. "Peace, Roberre. She's a friend."

The robot dog turned his head toward me. "Woof?"

I nodded. "Woof."

With a huff, Roberre sat back on his haunches. He did not scoot back, though.

I climbed the rest of the way up and motioned Taft to come up but stay behind me. That put the three of us crowded into the corner.

I squatted beside Earl's dog. "Roberre, this is Sam, and that's Taft. They're friends."

He sniffed at Taft then Sam. "Woof."

I hoped that did it. I pulled Taft off to the side behind me. Then I pointed at the ladder. "Go down there, boy. Guard the equipment."

"Woof!" Roberre trotted down the ladder—fortunately, the steep stair of a ship's ladder, not a vertical one like the one outside the airlock.

I let out a breath and rubbed my neck. "Sorry about that. I forgot he was here. And he's not my dog."

"Dog?" Taft stared, incredulous.

I shrugged. "Well, he *thinks* he's a dog."

Sam stepped away from the wall and the ladder, then gave me a sharp glance. "Who's dog is it?"

I started toward the corridor bridge. "We'd best get going. He belongs to my mechanic, Earl Cristo."

Sam's voice came from behind me. "Cristo? Oh, dear. And you separated him from Roberre?"

Beside the galley, I turned just as Taft came up behind Sam. "Jackson seemed to know him, too. What's the deal?"

Sam walked up to me, eyes a little wide as if she was afraid. "Back when I was an admiral, we saw some eyes-only files. Earl Montague Cristo is...dangerous."

Taft stopped in his tracks. "You were an admiral?"

Sam blinked then grimaced. I got the impression she'd reverted to being Brandy without noticing.

She turned, quite serious. "I was always a pilot first. And I'm a pilot now, *your* pilot."

This confirmed what she had now, a home. I'd never had a real place for myself since I'd left for New Zion and Solomon Tech.

I spread my hands. "I'm sorry, Taft, for breaking your peaceful home, but thank you for taking care of my big sister."

Sam scowled at me over her shoulder. "It needed breaking, or at least fracturing a little. I needed him to know. Let's go find Jackson."

With a nod, I opened the door to Jackson's quarters. "Taft, I don't have a third seat, so you'll need to lie on the bed. It may get uncomfortable, but don't get up unless I say so."

He frowned. "Okay."

He went to lie on the bed.

As we walked the few steps to the bridge, Sam took in the other quarters, the galley, and head. She grunted. "You have a cute little ship."

I stopped at the door to the bridge. "Cute?"

She chuckled. "Sorry. I'm just used to warships."

I walked on in and grabbed my helmet and tossed the spare to Sam. "Well, *Hiram's Revenge* can do things no warship can yet."

Sam caught the helmet and stared at it a moment. Then she shook herself and climbed gingerly into the recessed copilot's seat. "It's been thirty years since I wore one of these. Who's Hiram?"

I sat, buckled up, and jacked in. "My first love. It's a long story."5

While Sam got situated, I powered on the *Revenge*. Then I piped the Virtual Vision onto all six surfaces of Taft's room, even if it might be a bit disorienting.

Taft laughed. "That's...strange."

Sam sighed and flipped on the bridge intercom so only I could hear. "He thinks he understands, but he doesn't. He's going to be mad. It will take time, but he'll get used to it when he sees I'm not leaving." She snorted. "It takes him time to do everything. It took almost a year after we were close enough to ask me to move in with him. It's part of what makes him so comfortable to be around."

I lifted the *Revenge* off the ground. "Sorry."

Sam reached over and swatted my shoulder. "Stop apologizing. I've wanted to tell him for years." She put her hands on the joysticks, then took them off again. "When you broke the blockade, I know you bugged out in the atmosphere, but how did you even get down?"

Without changing our top-first, I gained altitude, angled us toward the twilight and thought about my answer. The *Revenge* crossed five thousand meters and headed toward ten. I wanted to show her, not tell her. She would love it.

I chuckled, wanting to surprise her with my Lu space antics. But I could show the simple stuff now. "I came in day to night, turned off my gravity drive, and used these."

I extended my control surfaces. We'd reached eight thousand meters, so I cut upward thrust. Then I banked into the strong twilight winds, caught a thermal and rose. Now we were flying front first.

"You've done that before," Sam said.

I wanted to laugh, or maybe cry. "That's a long story, too."

I turned us back toward the light and descended toward the higher passes. "We should try to sneak up on them."

I zigged-zagged down toward the light and between peaks where variegated rock peeked out through deep snow. In a slow descent, I approached the place Jackson had pinged from.

Before we crossed the last ridge, I powered on the laser turret.

Sam stirred. "It's been even longer since I've fired a weapon."

We cleared the stony escarpment below the icy peaks. A snowy valley opened before us, with a bare western face. But the valley was empty. Out over the middle, I stopped and turned the *Revenge* in a slow circle.

On the west face mine entrance gaped black down near the snow. And there were tracks from a ship's landing skids, plus footprints and maybe wheeled vehicles. Slag from the mine trailed down into the snow, purple rocky rubble.

I pointed, even though no one could see. "What kind of mine is that?"

"Sunstone!" Taft said, voice drifting in from the other room.

I reached out to ping Jackson's frequency again. "What are sunstones? And why would the Romans want them?"

Sam shrugged. "Semi-precious stones. I'd never seen them before I got here."

I got no response from my ping. "Well, damn. Jackson is gone. I guess we go higher."

The radio beeped, an incoming call from the space station.

I flipped open the channel. "This is Captain Lee."

"Captain Lee, we've received a call from Detective Bossen. He has an emergency with Earl, and he needs you ASAP. Meet him at the space port."

"Roger. We're on our way."

I tipped the nose up and punched it at four gs. "Hold on, Taft. This might be a rough ride."

8
EARL MONTAGUE CRISTO WAKES

I turned Hiram's Revenge away from our hunt for Jackson and toward Nyhagen and Earl. Worry for the big lug gripped my gut. I'd taken Roberre away. I'd turned Earl loose on the Romans. And I'd known he was dangerous.

Even so, I couldn't resist showing off and plotted a Lu space jump like I'd done on Earth to get to Beijing. When I hit the boost button, the *Revenge* jumped to five gs. The green light came on. I punched the button. The mountains stretched and faded into amorphic colors. Gravity eased off as the drives scaled back and we descended.

Sam swore. "What the hell?"

The world reappeared in a flash of light. My drives were still on. Nyhagen was off to the right, the space port below us. I decelerated hard and set the *Revenge* down gentle as a feather a hundred meters from any other ships.

"What the hell did you do?" Sam waved at the canopy. "That's not possible!"

I chuckled. "It is now. And that's how I got past the Roman blockade."

Sam jacked out and unbuckled. "I'm impressed."

I had just impressed Brandeis Clark. If it weren't for the specter of what I'd done to Earl, I'd have been walking on air.

Before I even powered down, three police cars screamed toward us.

I shut down the drives. Then I leaped from my seat and dashed for the back. I needed Roberre. When I reached the ladder, I realized Sam had not kept up. I looked back over my shoulder.

Sam moseyed down the corridor with a grin. "We're old and slow. Hurrying is not what we do anymore."

How old was she? I did some quick math and came up with a little over eighty. A shock of fear went through me. I would outlive her by a long way. Not now that I just found her!

At last, we made it down the ladder, and started the ramp down. Then, I turned back into the cargo hold. "Come, Roberre. We're going to see Earl."

Roberre trotted up to me. "Woof!"

Detective Bossen waited at the bottom with two other officers. "Captain Lee, please hurry."

I strode down. "We are coming as fast as we can. Also, you *will* leave guards around my ship. Shoot anyone that comes within twenty meters."

Bossen considered the size of *Hiram's Revenge*. "Um…I will get more men. Let's go."

By then, Sam and Taft had caught up with us, so we walked to the cars.

I lifted my bracer. "*Revenge*, close and virtual lock."

The driver got out to open the door and fairly jumped when she saw Roberre. "What is that?"

I let Roberre clamber in first, then paused with one foot inside. "What? Haven't you ever seen an emotional support dog?"

I got in the car and patted Roberre on the head. "Good dog."

"Woof."

Sam and Taft ended up in a different car, which I regretted, although it would give them time alone to deal with today's revelations.

Detective Bossen squeezed in beside me. That's when I noticed the bruise on his cheek. A chill went through me. What had Earl done?

After the driver closed the door he dashed around, got in, and peeled away, but without sirens. The other cars all got out of the way. They must have had an electronic warning system. How would I design such a thing? I had ideas, but the bumpy ride distracted me.

We drove at break-neck speeds back into the city and up to a printed building of gray stone that was way too small for a large city police department. It was just one story tall and only twenty meters wide. It had a parking lot next door with a garage big enough for a fleet behind. An ambulance pulled away as we drove in.

My heart sank into my belly. What had I done, not just to Earl, but the people of Eksil? They weren't ready for what had been unleashed upon them. Then again, the Romans had started this whole mess.

I turned to Bossen. "Detective, exactly what happened?"

Bossen shook his head in disbelief and regret. "Well, we went first to the hospital to interrogate the man with broken legs. Your Earl was forceful but also incisive. We found out the ship the man was from and that he was a pilot who'd been ordered to take your ship. However, when we got back here to do more research on the ship itself, the ship's captain showed up and demanded we allow him to take his man back, and that we had no authority to hold him.

"I got the captain down to one of our interrogation rooms, more of a conference room, really. Earl towered over the man and asked how much the Romans were paying him or if he were in fact himself a Roman spy. Then Earl walked away a moment, muttering to himself. I asked a few more questions. When Earl returned, he walked right over to the captain, yanked him to his feet and shoved him against the wall. When I tried to stop him, I got this."

Bossen tapped his cheek that was already purple. "After that, tings got bad. What Earl was saying made no sense, and he attacked the captain. It tog five officers to restrain him. Now we cannot calm him down again."

The driver parked and opened the door for us. Roberre managed to be the first one out. I ran after him, to a side door into the police station. Roberre had his paws up on the door, scratching to get in.

I patted his head. "Be calm. Go slow. And get down so I can open the door."

Roberre went down on all fours. "Woof."

When Bossen got there, I backed away to let him lead us.

He opened the door and strode in. Roberre surprised me by not running ahead.

Inside, the front corner of the station was an open area with murals of desert scenes on the walls. There were computer stations around the outside walls with cubicles for a little privacy. A counter ran diagonally opposite the corner and one officer waited there, talking calmly to a citizen.

Bossen took a left, deeper into the building, past offices. At the end of the corridor, he went through another door and down a flight of stairs. The walls here faded to dark gray, and the lights grew dim. In the hallway at the bottom, six officers stood watching a door as if it might attack them. Several had bruises or blood splattered on uniforms.

The corridor had a concrete floor, and doors and windows into the rooms on one side. Halfway down, there was an alcove with a guard station. Behind the guard station was another reinforced door. I assumed the jail cells were back there.

Bossen walked up to the officers. "Status!"

A tall young man with black hair shrugged. "Nothing much, sir. It's been quiet. Maybe the dream time is hjælper."

Roberre and I stepped up beside Bossen. "Dream time?"

He gestured toward the door. "We turned the lights out."

Fear gripped my stomach as Sam and Taft started down the stairs. Maybe I was wrong about which sister would die first. But I had made this problem.

Taking a deep breath, I laid my hand on the doorknob. "Come on, Roberre."

He padded over. "Woof."

I nodded toward Bossen. "Turn on the lights."

One of the officers flipped a switch. I turned the knob and stepped in. Blood splattered the dark gray walls. The lone table had been turned over. Two chairs lay broken into pieces, scattered across the floor.

With a yell, Earl surged up from the corner. He leaped toward me, death in his eyes. "No more!"

Roberre dashed into the room. "Ar-roof!"

Everyone stopped.

Even Earl. He stared at his hands in horror. They were covered with blood. "Captain? I...what happened?"

He dropped to the ground, and Roberre nuzzled him. Earl grabbed his robot dog and held on for life.

I took some deep breaths to calm down. The room reeked of sweat and blood and fear.

Sam stepped up behind me and leaned close. "Maybe it's been long enough. Order him to report and use his full name."

Hoping I hadn't broken him permanently, I stood at parade rest, feet spread, hands clasped behind my back. "Earl Montague Cristo, report!"

He snapped to his feet and came to attention, except for the one hand on Roberre's head. "Yes, Captain." Then he frowned. "Except, my name isn't Earl, or it wasn't. I...they...caught me. Pain. So much pain. So much blood. Make them...make them...pay. I'm so sorry."

The Earl I knew was calm and placid. This man radiated danger and fear and sorrow. He could and had killed with his bare hands.

I gave Earl a nod of approval, and then I stepped back over to Bossen and his officers. "Does anyone have a sunstone?"

A female officer pulled a ring off and handed it to me.

It had a silver setting and a translucent yellow stone. I weighed it in my hand. "You probably won't get this back."

She shrugged and pointed at Earl. "If it fixes *him*, it's worth it."

"We'll see."

I turned to Earl. He could snap me in two if he wanted. He'd called me captain, though. Swallowing the fear, and with slow, easy steps I approached this unhinged killer.

I showed him the ring. "If you want revenge on the Romans, find out why they want these."

When I pressed the ring into his palm, Earl blinked. He held it up to the light, puzzled. "Does it do something besides look pretty?"

Detective Bossen answered from the doorway. "I think it's used in certain computers."

Earl's expression slowly returned to its ordinary passivity, although I thought I detected a trace of emotion. Relief maybe, or curiosity.

He put the ring in his pocket. "A light computer perhaps? Energy transmission properties. I will need my equipment on the ship."

I nodded. "Then you will have it." I turned to Detective Berrins. "Is Earl free to go?"

He rubbed his neck and frowned. "Um, I'm not sure. He did assault that ship captain, nearly killed him."

Sam leaned close again. "Earl was a spy against the Romans. They caught him and tortured him."

That fit, but it didn't answer what the Council or the navy had done to fix him or make him into Earl. I needed to concentrate on the next steps, though.

I stepped back to the door. "I need three things. First, let Earl get cleaned up. If Roberre is with him, he'll be fine. Second, I would like to formally request that he be released into my custody, since he is a member of my crew. And third, see if you can get Rådmand Balbuk. I need to speak with him."

A few minutes later, I sat in the conference room next door with Sam and Taft beside me, all on one side of the table. The room had the same table, same gray walls as the one Earl had destroyed, and I presumed the same chairs, though the six in here had not been smashed.

Taft seemed to be brooding, not quite as placid about Sam's secret as he had at first, just as Sam had suggested. He still let Sam hold his hand.

Sam cuffed my shoulder. "You're here a couple days and you're hanging around with the Rådgivere?"

I chuckled. "Around here, I'm more famous than you."

She turned one hand up and nodded gravely. "I am content."

I would be, too, if I hadn't broken Earl, and Jackson wasn't missing.

Detective Bossen led Earl and Roberre into the room, along with an armed guard. Earl, neat and clean, had returned to his normal placid self, but for his haunted eyes.

He sat next to me. I reached out and laid a hand on his shoulder. "Are you okay?"

Earl shrugged. "I remember things that are not good, but I think I am okay for now. Thank you, Captain."

I thought that gracious since I'd gotten him into that mess.

Before I could answer, Razzy walked in. He and Bossen sat opposite the rest of us, though the guard remained standing.

Razzy cocked his head. "Hej. I begin to think you don't make entrances; you make waves."

A smile crept to my lips as I shrugged. "It runs in the family."

He spread his hands. "What can I do for you ret this minute? Did you finde Jackson?"

"Well, Sam and I found where Jackson was, but they seemed to have left. Before we could gain altitude and ping the beacon again, we got called to come back here. But we did find out what the Romans are after."

I gestured to Taft. "Tell them what you saw."

"Um, me?" Taft said, eyes wide like an animal caught in a floodlight.

Razzy smiled at Taft and leaned toward him. "An explorer and prospector like you, Taft? We always need your assistance."

He'd done the research on who was here before he came in. Was this how it worked when you chose the most competent people to head the government?

Taft seemed taken aback, but he held Razzy's gaze. "The mine had the purple slag of sunstone ore."

Razzy rubbed his chin. "Hmm. The Romans are after sunstones? Why? We use them in optical computers. How valuable would that be?"

I thought back over my engineering classes on computer hardware. Light computers tended to be a little bigger but were immune to electromagnetic interference and didn't mind heat. In other words, they had uses but not enough value for the effort and expense the Romans had put into this operation. Nor would it justify the risks the Romans were taking.

I shook my head. "Not at the price the Romans seem willing to pay. There's more. I'm hoping Earl can figure that out, if I'm allowed to take him to my ship with me."

Razzy raised a hand. "That is still under discussion." He turned his attention to Earl and pointed over his shoulder to the other room. "Earl, are you dangerous? Will what happened in there a little bit ago happen again?"

Earl knitted his brow. "Sir, I am unsure. I think, if Roberre is with me, I will be fine, although I am remembering a different life. If you are not a spy from Nova Roma, I will not harm you."

Razzy cocked his head. "Are you certain that captain was a spy from Nova Roma?"

Earl nodded. "Yes, sir. At the least he was paid off by them to have him bring spies here. That is close enough."

Detective Bossen squirmed in his chair. "You attacked my people when they tried to stop you."

Again, Earl just nodded. "I did. They tried to stop me from extracting information from a Nova Roman spy. I did not kill any of them when I could have. I wish...that I did not know how to kill with my hands."

Bossen scowled and shook his head but addressed Razzy. "Sir, it is my job to protect our citizens, and this man is dangerous. I do not like the idea of having him loose."

The man had a point, but I needed Earl. It was also my fault this happened. I opened my mouth to speak, but Earl beat me to it.

He raised his right hand. "I will give you my word not to leave the *Hiram's Revenge* while we are on Eksil. And I will keep Roberre with me always."

Bossen let out a big breath and frowned. "I will accept that, for now. It may change when we get the dommer involved."

I assumed a dommer must be a judge or magistrate, meaning this was far from over. Still, they'd agreed to let me take Earl with me. Time to change the subject.

I raised a finger. "One more thing. How do we prevent the Roman merchants from getting away with any more sunstones?"

Razzy ran a hand through his hair. "I'm not sure. They legitimately traded for the items."

Sam stirred and leaned forward. "Close the port."

Razzy pulled back, startled. "What? But that would mean..."

Sam gave a hand shrug. "Tell them the law has changed and they aren't allowed to trade here anymore, and do it to all of them, not just the spies."

Of course. Then it made sense. I pointed at Razzy. It was his job. "She's right. You need to confiscate what they purchased and give them back what they spent to get it. Oh, and get the destroyer *Lexington* to hover above the space port so none of them will try to leave while you're doing all this. Let them leave when you've made sure there are no sunstones on board."

Razzy leaned back and tapped the table. "That is a drastic course of action."

I chuckled then yawned. "We could go with a military blockade instead."

Razzy waved that off. "Yeah, but then some hotshot pilot would kom and break it." He thought it over a moment. "I will need to sige with the Overst Rådmand, but we will likely take your suggestion."

With that, he stood. "Now, I suggest you get Earl back to your ship and get some sleep. We'll know more when you wake."

Detective Bossen arranged a large car to take the five of us, including Roberre, back to the *Revenge*. I worried about Jackson but kept yawning.

Earl, still with one hand on Roberre's head, cleared his throat, "I'm sorry, Captain. I lost control."

I reached over and laid a hand on his knee. "No, Earl, it was my fault. I apologize to you for not letting Roberre come with you."

Earl frowned. "I think, perhaps it might be time for me to remember, at least in part."

9
DECOYS

The intruder alarm on the Revenge woke me. It automatically locked the doors to my quarters and enabled my virtual security protocols. It also locked Sam and Taft's door. I couldn't believe the Romans were trying again with all of us on board.

I pulled my helmet from under my bed and put it on. When I jacked in, I brought up a virtual keyboard. I wanted to see what these guys would do before Earl and Roberre got to them. I definitely needed to update the security on the airlock. I just hadn't had time to cover it all.

The security cameras showed three people, two women and one man, coming in through the airlock door. One of the women had a computer out, typing as she went. When I checked, her security bot was already into my virtual control machine, the one that had no link at all to the ship itself.

The other two carried a large machine, half a meter on a side, with ports and electrical connections. When they turned to wrestle the contraption down the ladder, I realized what it had to be—a gravity drive.

If they could get that hooked up to power, they could make it appear I flew the ship away.

There was one way to prevent that. *My* drives had more power.

I tapped my bracer. "*Revenge* on!"

My bracer formed virtual joysticks, detecting hand movements. I lifted the *Revenge* a foot off the ground. Then I opened a channel to the space port. "Eksil control, this is

Hiram's Revenge. We have been boarded again. There's an attempted hijacking in progress. So far, I am still in control."

"Roger, *Hiram's Revenge*. I will alert the police. Is there anything else we can do?"

I thought a bit. The woman with the computer dashed for the bridge. I retracted the furniture in the common room into the floor. Then I tipped the *Revenge* left onto its side. I hung vertical from my bed, feet down. The acceleration netting held me in place. Computer-woman in the corridor fell into the head.

The device in the common room tumbled across the deck. The Engineer-woman wrestling the tiny drive fell after it. The man ended up draped across the hatch to the lower deck.

I wondered if I could collect them. I rolled the *Revenge* the other way, putting my head down. The woman fell out of the head and up against my door. The little drive fell back across the common room. It took Engineer-woman with it. She screamed as she tried to get out of the way.

Before she reached the wall, I flattened the *Revenge* and tipped the nose up. Computer-woman slid down the corridor. I thought about opening the airlock doors but decided against it.

I flattened the *Revenge* and set it down again. "Earl, Roberre, now."

While the three thieves got to their feet, Roberre charged up the ladder. He barreled into the intruders. Roberre's charge distracted them enough that Earl made it up the ladder.

Earl, with exquisite calm, tossed computer-woman into engineer- woman. The man drew a pistol. Earl slapped his wrist. The man dropped the gun. Into Earl's hand. In a flash, Earl had it pointed at the man's head.

"Down!"

Computer-woman tried to draw a weapon. Roberre stepped on her arm. It snapped. He stepped on her computer, too.

While Earl tied up the three of them, I called space port control. "Eksil control, this is *Hiram's Revenge*. We have captured the intruders. Please, send the police."

"Roger, *Hiram's Revenge*, the police should already be there."

"Roger, roger. *Revenge* out."

I opened the rear airlock doors and released the acceleration netting. Then I took off my helm and got up to meet the police.

When I stepped into the corridor, Sam came out, steadying Taft.

Taft chuckled and shook his head. "Now I know you're related." He pointed a thumb at Sam. "This one tog the last young hotshot through downtown in the game jets."

They didn't have hugely tall buildings, but tight and tall enough that it would be right-angled corners.

Sam gave him a playful shove. "He doesn't like it when I go upside down."

A commotion at the rear drew our attention. The police made it up the ladder. When Sam, Taft, and I made it to the end of the corridor, Earl had the table and chairs extruded in the common room. He sat, leaning back, the assailant's gun on the table as far from his own hands as he could put it. Roberre sat on his haunches guarding the three prisoners against the wall near the ladder.

Two officers appeared in the airlock and stepped inside. Detective Bossen followed.

I put my hands on my hips. "Are you the only detective in the police force?"

He snorted. "They just know how much I like you."

He waved to his officers to take the prisoners away and used gloves to pick up the gun himself. "Is this theirs?"

Earl nodded toward the male prisoner. "I took it from him."

Bossen cocked his head. "You seem calm."

Roberre trotted over. "Woof."

A slow, rare smile spread across Earl's face. "What he said."

I stepped over to the device, which sat cock-eyed against the back wall, and pointed at it. "Detective. You will want this. I believe it is a small gravity drive." Then I realized how the intruders had gotten past the police cordon. "They may have ridden it to get here to bypass your guards. They planned to use it to steal the ship, since I'd locked out the ship's gravity drives."

Bossen stepped over and examined the mini drive. "I finde the timing curious. The *Lexington* is due overhead in one hour."

Sam chuckled. "You, detective, have a leak."

Bossen scowled. "I know, and I'm trying to figure out who and how." After a moment, he shook his head and met my gaze. "Are you going to look for Jackson again?"

I nodded. "That's the plan. Are we free to lift off?"

He smirked then gave a dismissive wave. "You have not traded for anything here. You are free to go."

I gave him half a salute. "Then we will search for Jackson and see what that mountain mine can tell us."

It took time for the police to gather the prisoners, the *Revenge*'s logs, and the portable gravity drive. After that, Sam and I strapped into the cockpit one more time. I fired up the gravity drives and got clearance from space port control. They even let the *Lexington* know I was authorized.

I lifted off and took the *Revenge* north and into the twilight. I caught a thermal over the ocean to take us even higher.

Sam shook her head. "I have so missed flying gravity drives."

"Want to fly it?"

I wasn't sure if I wanted her to or not. *Hiram's Revenge*, not a warship, wouldn't be the same as what she'd flown so long ago. Then again, I wanted her to be impressed with my ship, impressed with me.

Sam sounded wistful when she spoke. "Oh, you tempt me, but later, when it doesn't matter."

In a cloud bank, I dipped farther into obscurity. Then I turned on my radar countermeasures. Being invisible, or least unnoticed, might be an advantage against Roman spy ships.

Once I reached ten thousand meters, I pinged Jackson's beacon again. It responded from a spot a thousand kilometers into the dark.

Sam pointed and nodded. "That's a good place to hide. Mountains, glaciers, and darkness, of course."

I turned the *Revenge* toward the beacon and accelerated at four gs.

My sensor showed a light plume farther away than an incoming ship should fall out of Lu space. It was also off to the side, almost directly over the twilight. Two more flashes followed, which would be the star sharks coming to check out the newcomer.

Then things got strange, all a light-minute behind reality. A radio broadcast came in. "This Captain Rodriguez of the *Defiant* out of Tanterra. The star sharks are attacking! Help!"

The reply came from the other destroyer in orbit. "This is the CPN *New Dehli*. You are not under attack. Do not fire!"

Sam stirred. "Too late, that's laser fire."

Light shot out from the *Defiant*, being much too defiant.

The *New Dehli* broke orbit, heading out to help.

This could be bad.

A ship lifted off from the dark. Right where Jackson's beacon pinged from. It headed out of the gravity well almost opposite of the *Defiant*'s inbound vector.

I opened a channel to the *New Dehli*. "This is *Hiram's Revenge*. The *Defiant* is a decoy. Break off."

With a growl, I punched the *Revenge* to four gs and chased the mine ship. Jackson's beacon still pinged from it. Based on her rate of climb, my quarry had drives as good as mine, but weighed down by the ore in her hold. The *Revenge* could accelerate faster. I tipped us further upward. Going through less atmosphere, and so fighting less air resistance, would enhance my advantage.

A few minutes later, as we left the atmosphere, I turned on my weapons and flipped fire control to Sam.

She turned her head, watching the crosshairs follow her gaze. "Huh. I've never been the fire control officer before." After a moment's pause, she added, "We aren't going to catch them before they jump."

Jackson was on that ship. They were not getting away.

10
SPACE DANCE

With the *Revenge* closing, the Roman spy ship carrying Jackson changed its vector to put distance between us.

I plotted a short jump.

"What's that line?" Sam asked, pointing at the graph in Virtual Vision.

Even after our little in-atmosphere jump, I wanted to impress my big sister. "It plots our ascent, or descent, into and out of Lu space. Watch this."

I hit the boost, then the jump button. The stars around us stretched and faded for just a moment. I turned the *Revenge* to come in across their bow. The weird colors of Lu space brightened, expanding into a light plume. The *Revenge*'s descent intercepted real space and we fell out, still under thrust.

"What the hell?" Sam said even as she targeted the spy ship's top laser turret. She fired.

The Roman's first laser turret shattered.

We crossed a hundred kilometers in front of them. Proximity alarms went off. Their automatic system backed off thrust to avoid a collision. I hadn't turned the avoidance system back on after Planeta De Angel.

The Roman veered off my vector and laid on the thrust again. It tipped sideways to fire at us with their bottom turret.

Sam launched chaff. Then she fired at the Roman's second turret.

I turned the *Revenge* to give chase. "Good thing that's a cargo ship."

I hit the boost and closed the distance. Then I cut across in front of the Roman again.

My Virtual Vision magnified weapons fire light-seconds away, out where the *Defiant* would be—firing at the star sharks again.

I continued the dance with the Jackson's ship.

The *New Dehli* jumped to close the distance with *Defiant*.

I cut across the Roman's bow again, slowing them.

Then, in a flash of light, the *Defiant* fell out. Heading right toward me. It fired two missiles.

Sam fired at the first missile. It exploded.

I hit the jump button.

The stars stretched and vanished.

I grimaced. "We're vastly outgunned."

The *Defiant* didn't seem to be a destroyer, but it clearly had more weapons than the *Revenge.*

Sam growled. "They're not getting away with Jackson."

I turned the *Revenge* around, still in Lu space. "Roger that."

Jackson had given me refuge at the academy, a refuge I desperately needed in that place I hadn't wanted to be.

I located both ships on gravity scan and flew past them. I turned again and fell out at an angle, cutting across the bow of the Jackson's unnamed ship. Again.

Their automatic collision alarm dropped their drives. Again.

The *Defiant* launched two more missiles at me. Sam fired as they came out of the launch bays. The *Defiant*'s lasers targeted the *Revenge*'s turret. Sam swore as her lasers vanished.

I dodged. Then moved a finger and touched the jump button.

As the stars stretched and faded, four more light plumes appeared. Star sharks!

The stupid *Defiant* had attacked them, and they'd followed it here. Now they were going to throw a wrench in the works.

"Oh, hell." I turned the *Revenge* around and went back.

We fell out again, strange colors stretching into a light plume. The four star sharks launched missiles at the *Defiant* and Jackson's cargo ship. Twelve missiles from the sharks flew toward the Roman ships. Two more came toward us.

The *Defiant* put itself between the sharks and the cargo ship. It fired four missiles, one at each shark. Then it tried to take out the shark missiles with its lasers.

Outnumbered and outgunned by the sharks, how could I save Jackson and stop the Romans from getting away, too, all without weapons?

I headed toward the sharks then cut between the two Roman ships. It forced the cargo ship to back off its thrust again.

Some of the shark's missiles closed on the *Revenge*. I jumped again. As the stars faded, the telltale prismatic haze enveloped all four sharks. They'd jumped, too.

For a moment, I let the *Revenge* get farther away, not moving the controls. "How can I stop star sharks destroying those ships and stop the Romans from getting away? I don't have any lasers or missiles!"

"I want my fighter!" Sam pounded the console beside her seat. "You did just right. Make the missiles follow you and lose them in Lu space, all while making the ship with Jackson slow down. Then we hope the *New Dehli* gets here in time."

I turned the *Revenge* around and settled into my seat. "Child's play compared to taking out four sharks in a jump fighter like you did."

Sam snarled. "I was angry. They'll come from behind this time."

Anger I knew, but if I got angry, I'd fly away and let them have Jackson. Because saving Jackson was doing just what the bastards who created me wanted.

I adjusted my vector. The *Revenge* fell out again, with drives still engaged. I cut across the unnamed freighter's bow. This time I flew above to below, angling back toward Eksil.

Three light plumes disgorged sharks behind and above the freighter, firing three missiles each.

I hit the boost button. The *Revenge* gave me five gs. I behind the freighter and dove toward the missiles.

Sam craned her neck, scanning the night skies. "Where's the other shark? There are two more harassing the *New Dehli* yonder, but those aren't any of our four."

The *Defiant* reversed thrust to intercept the missiles, same as me.

Three missiles followed me. The Defiant took two more with its laser cannons.

As the missiles closed in, I fretted. How long before they exploded? How long before they came into Lu space with me?

I hit the jump button. As the stars stretched, another light plume appeared. On the far side of the freighter from the others. The other shark!

"Damn it!"

I whipped the *Revenge* around. Could I get back soon enough? Without time to calculate, I dropped the drives. We fell out. The light plume faded to stars. Explosions lit the night.

The late-arriving shark had fired three missiles at the freighter. The *Defiant* was out of position to help. It turned toward the freighter anyway.

The two sharks, now behind the *Defiant*, fired more missiles at it.

The *Defiant* ignored the missiles behind. It fired lasers at the missiles targeting the freighter. It destroyed two.

Then the missiles from the other side hit the *Defiant*.

The last missile hit the freighter.

Both ships exploded. Silent flames spouted as the oxygen burned. Pieces of ships tumbled away into the night.

Neither Sam nor I spoke.

Jackson gone? How could that be?

Four star sharks, directly ahead of me, demanded my attention. They fired two missiles each.

I accelerated away, backwards. Restraints dug into my shoulders and hips as we took negative gs. I hit the jump button. A thought occurred to me: this wasn't the shark's fault. The *Defiant* had attacked *them*.

In Lu Space, I turned and went back. This time I went past the sharks and fell out. Again, I floated with my drives off.

Sam stirred. "What are you doing?"

"I don't know. Making peace?" I punched up the video of the star shark community out by the gas giant that I'd taken on my first trip to Eksil and flipped it over to Sam's Virtual Vision.

The here-and-now sharks moved toward me and fired one missile each.

I repeated my maneuver: jump, turn, fall out where no missiles were aimed.

Sam gestured wildly at the air in front of her. "Where did you get this video?"

Why was she upset? What did it have to do with her? Was it because she'd fought so many of them?

I shrugged. "I ran across them accidentally on my first trip here, when I rescued Rådmand Retts."

It took two more jumps before the sharks didn't fire any missiles at me. Then the five of us sat in space near each other, just watching.

"Now what?" Sam asked. "You know they killed Jackson, right?"

"What's going on out there?" Taft said over the intercom. He'd stayed quiet for the whole battle. "What are those?"

Sam scanned the stars overhead. "Those, my love, are the aliens that fly around the gas giant every few years."

"They wouldn't have killed Jackson if the *Defiant* hadn't attacked them to create a diversion. That was a stupid plan."

Sam snorted. "Really stupid, unless they'd had *me* in a warship."

"You fought those?" Taft said.

That drew a sigh from Sam. "I did. As far as we knew, they attacked us first. I've fought more of them than any other human pilot."

"Computer, search alien communication." I did the gravity drive equivalent of waggling my wings.

After a pause, one of the sharks waggled back at me, so I tipped my nose down and up, kind of like a wave. The shark imitated that maneuver, too.

Sam had asked another question. What now?

I had no idea. I wondered if I could display pictures outside my ship, planets and moons and stars. I had a holographic projector, but it was inside the ship. I might be able to use the laser turret if it hadn't been blown up again.

I brought up my virtual keyboard and started in. "Sam, waggle at them occasionally. I need to see if my hologram projector will point outside."

While I worked, Sam started with patterns. One waggle, two nods. Three waggles, one nod. Then a Fibonacci series in nods; one, one, two, three, five, eight. The shark responded, after a pause, with thirteen.

Sam did an entire spin, whistling as she did it. "It's been too long. I've missed flying starships."

Taft didn't say a word, which I thought was telling. He and Sam hadn't worked out their revised relationship yet.

About the time I figured I couldn't make a hologram outside, the sharks did flips and headed back toward the gas giant.

Sam did one more waggle. "We must have bored them."

I took the controls and turned to head back to Eksil. "We'll need to get some scientists out to work on that."

The radio crackled, the space station calling. "Hej, *Hiram's Revenge*. There is an emergency at the spaceport. Please return at best speed and land at the game master's house."

I flipped us around and headed back toward Eksil. "Roger. We'll be there shortly."

I tapped Sam's arm. "You want to fly it?"

She stirred as if waking. "Yes. Do we need to jump?"

I nodded. "That call makes me think a stealth entrance would be good. I say we come in low out of the twilight."

Sam put her hands on the joysticks. "You'll have to show me how to do your special jumps."

I shrugged. "Just plot a course. The computer does most of the work, though sometimes I do turns manually."

After bringing up the navigation software, Sam accelerated toward Eksil. She plotted a course with an ascent, then a turn and a descent. We'd fall out on the night side on a path toward the game complex rather than space port.

I didn't want her flying my ship. I wanted to do it myself. *Hiram's Revenge* was mine. I squashed that. This was my sister. I wouldn't let anyone *except* her fly it.

Sam gave me a sidelong glance. "Not easy giving up control? I get that. By the way, kid, you're a good pilot, but a better engineer, I think."

"Right. *I'm* a good pilot." I sounded bitter. I was bitter. And angry.

Sam laid a hand on my shoulder. "You are a *good* pilot. Not as good as I used to be, but I was obsessed, and I paid a big price for that obsession."

I snorted. "But I'm supposed to be just like you, the second coming of the great Brandeis Clark."

She smacked my arm then hit the jump button. "Who says? You've done more with this ship than I ever dreamed. But you know what? I need to hear your story. What was your life like growing up?"

The stars stretched and faded. We left the universe into a lonely place by ourselves.

Where to begin? Then I remembered and closed my eyes. "Is Jackson really gone?"

11

EXTORTION

Sam growled as we approached fallout twenty seconds later. "It's just not like Jackson to even be on that ship at all."

I waved back where we'd just been. "Why was he trying to play spy at his age? Unless..."

Sam glanced over. "What?"

The muted colors stretched and brightened into a light plume. Eksil appeared just below us, dark and snowy. Sam tilted the nose up and decelerated into the atmosphere.

I shook my head and extended the control surfaces. It was all so absurd. "Unless the bastards that created me got to him. And they wanted me in on this for some reason."

Sam messed around with the heads up displays. "How could they get to him after he retired? Hmm. You've used your new adaptation to lower your ascent into Lu Space, but have you increased it?" She made an upward swooping motion. "Maybe go straight up?"

The thought hadn't even occurred to me. I'd been using it for exceedingly practical missions, not trying to experiment, so I shrugged. "No. Maybe later we can try."

Sam dropped down into the darkness through the bumpy air. She used the wind to go where she wanted. "At least it doesn't *fight* the wind. Why did you add the control surfaces?"

I snorted. "When I picked up Ambassador Retts, I used a decoy missile, shut down my drives, and glided in."

With a glance at me, Sam took the drives to zero thrust. My stomach leapt into my throat.

"Whoa!" Taft said.

After a minute or two, Sam turned the thrust back on and continued deceleration.

Then she shook her head. "Glide? I think that would be a moderated fall."

She brought us in low. My hands still wanted to be on the joysticks. By the time we reached the twilight, we'd crossed below a kilometer. Sam banked around a mountain and dropped down over a precipice.

After that, we cruised over the plain south of the city toward the game complex a hundred meters off the ground. I glanced toward the spaceport and found the Lexington hovering high overhead, maybe ten thousand meters. That was higher than launch-prevention would usually be, at least if I were in charge.

Sam landed the *Revenge* soft as a feather, right where I'd parked earlier. Three police cars waited on the road.

I lowered the ramp even as Sam powered down.

Moments later, Sam, Taft, and I walked down the ramp. Razzy, Vada, Detective Bossen, and five other officers emerged from Vada's house and headed across to meet us. We'd left Earl and Roberre on board, as promised.

Whatever was going on, Razzy stayed in the background with Vada.

Detective Bossen strode forward and put his hands on his hips, feet spread. "You make life too exciting for me. The traders have refused to give the merchandise back."

That didn't sound good. With the *Lexington* hovering overhead, the spies had to have some leverage they thought would get them out of here.

I closed my eyes, dreading the answer. "What did they do?"

Bossen's drawl was chilling. "They threatened to blow up the city."

A chill went through me. I suddenly wanted to be back on the *Revenge* somewhere above the *Lexington*. No wonder it was so high. My eyes flew open, and I pointed toward the spaceport. "They're claiming to have a nuke? Can we verify that?"

Bossen shook his head and made a dismissive wave. "All the ships claimed to have a nuke."

I scowled at how unlikely that was. "A ship hired by the Romans wouldn't have a nuke. Only a ship actually from Nova Roma would."

Sam paced behind me. "I agree. But if they did set it off, there would be another war. It's a huge risk."

Just then, Vada's two older kids burst from the house. Gamila held a squirming Damien, but reached out a hand to stop the other two. It was too late.

Tamara went to stand with Vada, trying to appear serious, as if she belonged. Dural dashed forward and ducked under Razzy's arm. Razzy tousled his hair.

The two of them kind of looked alike. Surely Razzy wasn't his father. Had he been with Vada? He didn't live with her. What did that mean?

Razzy broke my train of thought as he stepped forward through the officers. "Perhaps it would merely be a huge risk for Nova Roma, but Eksil would effectively be gone."

Fear settled in my guts. I liked these people and this strange place. I had more friends here than anywhere else except maybe Thurman.

I thought about what I'd seen from orbit. At least three quarters or their population lived near the city. A nuke here, and Razzy was right, Eksil would be gone.

Sam stepped up and laid a hand on my shoulder. "Let them go. At least tell them you're letting them go."

Razzy cocked his head. "What do you mean?"

She pointed at the bright sky. "The *Lexington* and the *New Dehli* should be able to shoot them all down in orbit."

Bossen and Razzy both glanced upward, doubtful, and I immediately knew why; if one of those ships got a missile off, Eksil was gone.

I pointed up at the speck that was the *Lexington*. "But who's going to stop the missiles...?"

Sam followed where I'd pointed. "You have chaff?" She thumbed at the *Revenge*.

I turned to face Sam, waving my arms as fear tightened my gut. I did not want her to be right. "You want to put *us* between those ships and the city? Without a laser cannon?"

She glared, with steel in her eyes, but her voice was almost a whisper. "Yes."

Damn it, she was right. I turned toward Razzy and
Bossen, who had watched in silence. I only saw the terror in
their eyes as they watched Sam and me. I opened my mouth
to plead with them to find a different idea. Instead, I whirled
to face *Hiram's Revenge.* "Earl!"

"Yes, Captain?" He strode part way down the ramp and
ducked to see me.

I pointed at the top of the *Revenge.* "I need that laser
turret fixed. Now!"

Sam laid a hand on my shoulder. "Thank you. This is my
home."

I thought about how hard I would fight for *Hiram's
Revenge* and realized what she meant. I nodded toward the
ship. "I understand."

Earl, meanwhile, was clambered up to the top of the
Revenge. I could hear the printer inside starting on repair
parts. How did he do that?

I raised my voice, as he reached the top. "And print us
more anti-missile chaff."

"Yes, Captain."

Razzy put hands on hips, but his gaze followed Earl. "And
I will negotiate for another hour or two." Then he smiled. "I'll
say the destroyers are angry about the threat and we're trying
to convince them. In fact, I will *actually* have to convince
them."

I yawned. "I need to get some sleep." Others agreed, and
the party started breaking up.

Then I had another thought: fight for my home.
"Detective, could you lend me some officers? As soon as we're
ready, I'll take the *Revenge* over to the space port. The
Romans will want to steal it, and they may delay any other
actions until they try."

Sam nodded; lips pursed. "Dangerous, but a good idea."

Vada came around then, touching hands and arms. "We
have food inside. Come, let us eat while we wait."

No one seemed excited, and once inside we loaded up
food buffet-style off the counter in the kitchen, no one spoke
much. Razzy, who'd made some calls before getting in line,
wolfed down his food and rose. As he went toward the door,
he waved me over.

I followed him outside. "What's up?"

He gave me a worried smile and took both my hands. "I wanted to thank you for agreeing to hjælp us. Takker dig. I am pleased and grateful."

I wanted to go back to joking with him. It was much more fun, though his warm hands almost made me blush. It had been a long time since anyone had shown an interest in me. I winked at him. "My sister does live here."

That produced a real, if ironic, grin. "You didn't do it for me at all?"

I stepped a little closer. He had not relinquished my hands. "You? You have nice eyes, but is that any reason to risk life and limb to avoid a nuclear catastrophe?"

His competence and self-assurance, not to mention his sense of humor, attracted me much more anyway. I certainly didn't want to share him with Vada.

"Well then." He leaned in for a gentle kiss on my lips. "Know that you are always welcome here, for a visit or for longer."

I got the feeling that was a personal invitation rather than a general one, which intrigued me.

Before I could answer, Sam and Taft walked out.

Sam touched my shoulder. "We'd best go."

The three of us started for the ship, and I turned to walk backward and smiled at Razzy. I didn't know where this would lead, but it was fun. "We'll talk more later."

We climbed the ramp to the cargo deck as two police officers dashed up behind us, a tall, wiry woman, and a wide man with thick black hair. I glanced back at them. "Best find a seat and buckle up."

Earl had his tools and equipment arranged so it almost formed a makeshift barrier. Behind that he'd strung a zero-g hammock with acceleration netting, and the laser turret sat near the 3D printer.

Earl peered out from his cordoned area. "Hello, Captain. How are we doing?"

"Just get us the laser cannons back. We're the planetary missile defense system." I turned the corner and clambered up the ladder. Sam and Taft followed more slowly, by the time Sam sat down virtual-Hiram's seat and Taft got into his cot, I'd finished the pre-flight checks. Then I yawned in my helmet.

I didn't want to fly anywhere. I wanted to sleep. But we needed to be obvious, where the Roman spies could see us. I lifted *Hiram's Revenge* off the ground and headed into the twilight without gaining much altitude at all.

Sam glanced back over her shoulder. "Trying to hide where we came from?"

"That's the idea."

Once we crossed into darkness and out of sight and of gravity sensor range, I gained altitude. Then I circled back, came down to the spaceport tarmac, and took my place at the end of the line. I shut the *Revenge* down and then getting up seemed more effort than it was worth. I could sleep in the pilot's seat. I could.

Sam removed her helmet and rolled to her feet. Then she held out her hand. "Come, Sister. You'll sleep better in your bunk."

With a sigh, I took her hand and got up. I swear I was asleep before I got to my bed.

★★★★★

Ka-boom

I was out of bed in my cabin before I registered what woke me. That explosion had been close, inside the ship maybe.

Breathing hard, I scrambled for my helmet, jumped back in my bunk, and jacked in. This is what we wanted. But what were the spies trying now?

Once the Virtual Vision came up, I found the internal monitors. Three men dashed in through the remains of the rear airlock. Two had heavy bags and one carried a gravity lift. They hustled down the ladder to the cargo deck.

The two police officers they'd left me emerged from the galley and headed back. The man reached the ladder and started down. A shot from below stopped him. Blood splattered. He fell back. With a shoulder wound.

I started to power up the drives.

The female officer fired down the ladder. Then she gave a quick peek.

Roberre barked and growled.

I used the Virtual Vision to peer through the floor. All three intruders froze as Roberre dashed out from behind

Earl's equipment. Two of them shot at the robot dog. To little effect.

The female officer fired again and slid down the ladder.

Roberre charged. Earl dove over the equipment. A punch to the throat from Earl took down the first spy. Roberre ran into the second one's legs. There was an audible crack. The second spy screamed.

The female officer put her gun to the third spy's head before he could even glance her way.

My radio crackled. I opened the channel there in my cabin.

A woman's voice said, "This is Eksil Spaceport Control. Detective Bossen says an agreement has been reached. Cargo ships will be cleared to leave shortly."

I brought up the airlock camera in Virtual Vision. The inner and outer door were both blown. And we didn't have a laser turret either. We couldn't fly. We couldn't shoot down any missiles.

"Roger, Eksil Control. See if you can slow down departure approval. And send Detective Bossen to my ship."

The woman laughed. "We will try, but they are eager to be away."

I ripped off the helmet and dashed out into the corridor. There I stopped, staring at the hole in my ship, my only home, such as it was. And I was about to be stuck on the ground while the city was under attack. My heart sank to my feet.

Then the anger flared. They'd damaged Hiram's ship. That would not stand. Time to be a captain.

I grabbed the med kit from the galley. "Sam! Taft! We need to move!"

I dashed back to the common room, still set up with the tiny dining table, to find the male officer on the floor, against the wall near the hatch down to the cargo deck with his hand over his shoulder wound. I knelt beside him. "Thanks for your help."

He snorted. "I was not nyttig, even a little."

This was outside my area of expertise, but I was being the captain now, so I imagined what Razzy or Bossen might say. Being a captain on a one-person ship meant a lot of jobs. "Nonsense. You distracted them just enough that Roberre could attack. And sacrificed your body to do it."

He looked into my eyes. "Takker dig."

I winked and pulled his shirt open. "Let's get this patched until a real medic gets here." I hoped it would be Razzy. I retrieved a self-sealing pressure bandage from the med kit and slapped it on the wound. Then I patted his other shoulder. "I think you'll live. If you can get down the ladder, that would be excellent."

He gave me a half-smile, half-grimace, and I helped him to his feet. He saluted with his left hand and hobbled down the ladder.

Sam and Taft stepped into the common room, rumpled and rubbing their eyes, but Earl needed instructions first, so I raised a hand for them to wait.

I lowered the cargo ramp with my bracer. Then I yelled down to the cargo deck. "Earl! Get the prisoners to the bottom of the ramp. Then get that laser turret back on top of the ship. If you can make it appear you're trying to repair the airlock, that would be ideal."

Earl's voice floated back up, sounding like his usual calm self, which meant Roberre was nearby. "Yes, Captain."

I straightened up and pointed at Sam. "Go on down and see if they need help with the prisoners. Get all of them off my ship. Taft, you and I are going to board up the back door." I thumbed at the airlock.

Taft seemed taken aback. "Um, how?"

I clasped his shoulder. "I'll show you. Ambassador Retts was able to help. You can, too."

I led Taft down the ladder and Sam followed.

When we emerged below, the ramp was almost down. Earl glared at the three intruders with Roberre right beside him. The female agent bound their wrists and ankles.

I hopped down onto the top of the ramp and dashed over to the engineering station across from the ladder. There, I retrieved the molecular grinder and went back across to hand it to Taft, who'd at last reached the bottom.

He was staring at the intruders and the blood, eyes wide, shaken by the violence. Why wasn't I shaken by all this? Because I had tasks to accomplish, and I'd lived on Angel's Planet for a few years.

I handed Taft the grinder. "Hold this end over the rough parts on the inside wall. Push the red button. Don't get your fingers on the working side. We just need it smooth enough to make a seal.”

Taft, stood on the bottom step of the ladder and turned the grinder over in his hand, careful to keep the business end away from him. “And how smooth is that?”

Held my hand up, fingers a little bit apart. “No more than a centimeter on the inside wall. Don’t worry about the airlock itself or the outside. I need to get some panels off the ceiling, which I will need help to wrestle up the ladder.”

First, though, I scampered back to the engineering station and queued up airlock replacement parts for the 3D printer to work on later. Then I grabbed a few tools and started prying some ceiling panels loose.

Outside, I heard cars pull up, which I assumed were the police. The high-pitched whine of a gravity drive powering up also reached my ears. The first trader/spy was preparing to leave. From the sound, so far only one.

I paused a moment. If spaceport control was restricting lift-offs to one at a time, they would want them all off before the first reached firing range for those destroyers.

Taft and I wrestled two narrow ceiling panels up the ladder and through the hatch and placed them against the *Revenge*’s broken aft wall. By that time, Earl had rigged a long tarp hanging from where the laser turret would go down over the airlock, or the hole where it had been.

After that, Taft and I strung the wire lattice from the repair kit around the outside. The whole process reminded me of creating that heat shield across the front strut when I took Ambassador Retts to Earth, in other words, work the makers of the repair kit had never imagined.

At last, the two of us stood drenched in sweat and with a blank wall panel where the *Revenge*’s back door should have been.

Now, with the matrix in place, I hit the button on the hull repair wand to dispense the foam. The tan stuff expanded in and around the lattice.

Taft poked a little of the foam with his finger, making a dent. “How is this supposed to seal anything?”

I laid a hand on his shoulder and presented the wand. “Push that button.”

Taft did, and the foam hardened, which sealed the panels to the interior wall. Fortunately, as we got to higher altitudes, the internal atmospheric pressure would hold the panel against the wall.

Sam came upstairs with the bag one of the intruders had been lugging. "I hate being bait. At least that's over."

Taft gave her a peck on the lips as Sam dropped the bag on the table.

She rummaged through it and pulled out a gravity lift and some cutting tools. "I think they were planning to steal your entire gravity drive."

I stepped over to look at the tools, then shook my head. "They would have been surprised at what they didn't get."

Sam glanced back at the hatch, then toward the bridge. "Ah! A multi-part solution. That figures. Is Earl done?"

I used my bracer to open a channel to Earl's earbud. "Hey, Earl. How's the installation?"

His disembodied voice came back. "Almost done, Captain. The last cargo ship just launched."

At the same time, my bracer beeped with an incoming message, which I answered. "This is Deuce."

A gravelly voice came on, calm and detached. "This is the *Lexington*. You have seven minutes before we open fire."

"Roger, *Lexington*. We'll get this crate airborne and lay down some chaff. *Hiram's Revenge* out."

We not only needed to be airborne, but we also needed some altitude before then, to make sure any explosions were high enough in the air.

I turned to head for the bridge. "Taft, get strapped in. Sam, you're with me again. Earl, get that tarp down and let's get off the ground."

I strode to the bridge. Sam followed more slowly behind. The sloped glass canopy and two seats were so familiar and so comforting I relaxed, but only until I realized Earl was not inside yet. I grabbed my helmet, sat, and jacked in.

I opened a channel. "Hello, Eksil Control. This is *Hiram's Revenge*. We'll launch momentarily. Please have the police pull back."

"Roger, *Hiram's Revenge*. You are cleared for launch. Hope we don't need your assistance."

Sam stepped onto the bridge and levered herself down into the copilot's seat while I went through the preflight checks and waited for Earl. What was taking him so long?

The Virtual Vision erased the bulk of the ship and enhanced radar and gravity scan into visible light images. The eleven spy ships spread out above me. The two destroyers loomed higher still. Earl was climbing down from atop the *Revenge*.

I tapped my knee. "Come on, Earl. Come on."

On the ground was the most dangerous place to be. I wanted altitude. Now!

Sam chuckled a bit and patted my arm. "Patience, child. We'll get there."

Even so, she activated the weapon system and scanned the skies for missiles.

I counted breaths. And imagined Earl's steps. Come on!

It seemed to take forever before Earl's voice came over the intercom with utter calm. "We are in. Go."

I punched the drive pedal to the floor. The Revenge responded with four-gs. The tarmac shattered. "Boost!"

One more g pushed me down into my seat. We gained altitude and gained on the last ship.

Above, the *New Delhi* fired on the first spy ship to launch. Laser fire followed by one missile.

The *Lexington* fired on the second ship. The other spies tried to scatter.

Seven of them fired missiles down toward the planet.

12
MISSILE DEFENSE SYSTEM

Seven missiles headed right toward us, toward the city. The *Revenge* rose toward the heavens, but the missiles came down faster. My stomach fluttered and sweat dripped down my sides. Every muscle was tight.

It felt like the eyes of a million people, hoping and praying they would not be obliterated in the next few minutes, were on me. And I was supposed to save them. With one puny little laser turret.

Sam looked up at the closest missile. The targeting system tracked her eyes. She fired.

It took three tries before the missile exploded.

Sam kept firing. Two more missiles vanished. The spies launched six more. We had ten to kill. We were losing ground. We were going to fail.

We couldn't wait. I turned to cross the city and dropped a radar-opaque chaff. I still gained altitude.

The spy ships continued to scatter, trying to make things harder for the two destroyers. I wanted to go shoot them all down, but I didn't have the weaponry.

Sam opened a channel to the two destroyers. "*Lexington* and *New Dehli*, this is *Hiram's Revenge*. These two ships will have the real nukes." She laced two of the ships with the lasers—one high up and one the next to last to leave.

Both of those fired two missiles each—two down at the planet, one each at the destroyers.

I dropped chaff, hoping we didn't run out. We'd printed up a lot more. "What did you see?"

Sam targeted the closest missile and fired. "They flat-shifted."

She was right. Small freighters, even ones as small as the *Revenge*, did not usually have bi-modulated fields. They always flew top-first and couldn't flat-shift. They might give that flexibility to a spy ship. I angled toward the lower of the two, the next to last to lift off.

Sam shot four more missiles, including the two from the spy ships.

We reached ten thousand meters. I hoped that was high enough that an air burst wouldn't destroy the city. I didn't know whether to turn left or right. The result was a wobble before I just reversed thrust and rotated the ship. I cut across the path of the missiles and laid chaff.

The *New Delhi* fired at two ships out over the dark.

When the first real spy ship cleared the atmosphere, it headed away southward at a shallow angle. The *Lexington* bored down on it. The second spy ship launched four missiles at once. Three of them upward, but not at either destroyer.

Sam shot at the down-bound missile. She didn't destroy it, just hit the control vanes. The missile spun off into the darkness.

Another missile hit the chaff and exploded.

The *Lexington* fired at the first spy ship and the missiles that the second spy ship had fired upward.

Sam destroyed another missile. She seemed to be getting faster and more accurate. "I've missed this. Tell me why you're so angry."

Still climbing, I released more chaff. "What? Why are you asking me that *now*?"

She nodded toward my joysticks. "I felt that wobble. You need to relax just a little. Don't think so much. Just do." She paused. "Why are you so angry?"

I willed my muscles, and my stomach, to unclench. They had other ideas. Those people down there were still depending on me. To survive.

With nothing better to do, I turned around to lay more chaff and answered. "It started the day before I went off to college on New Zion. That's when my parents told me about you being my sister."

An intense flash from off in the dark distracted us. Virtual Vision dimmed the light, so our eyes didn't burn. Moments later a wall of air washed over the *Revenge*. It pushed us sideways.

"That was a nuke!"

Sam looked up. "Oh, hell."

Another flash, just as bright, enveloped the space station.

As the afterimages faded, neither of us spoke. Rage built inside me.

I hit the jump button. The planet faded and reappeared. I'd fallen out with drives active, between the spy ship and the last freighter.

"Sam, fire at the one behind us first!"

She did as I asked. "What are you doing?"

I accelerated toward the spy ship. "What you did to that first star shark."

The bastards who created me wanted Brandy; this is what they got.

As soon as the ship behind fired a missile at us, Sam targeted the spy ship. She shot at its laser turrets.

The spy ship fired a missile at me.

"Incoming! Three seconds," Sam said.

I counted. One. Two. "Boost! Jump!"

The atmosphere faded away. The resultant void in the air would toss the two ships around. In Lu space, I turned back immediately. Everyone below was depending on me.

13
GAMES, STONES, AND STORIES

The colors of Lu space seemed to mirror my roiling mood. The seconds to get back to the battle above Nyhagen seemed like an eternity. I again wished I had missiles or just better weapons.

Sam shifted in her seat and touched my arm. "Until I met Taft, I would have said your parents did wrong by not telling you sooner. Now I know the indecision, the fear, the doubt. How can you reveal such a secret when it might destroy your family?"

It seemed a weird time to have a family talk. Then I noticed the intercom light on. She wanted Taft to hear. Thinking about family made me glad I'd reconciled with my parents.

The *Revenge* fell out lower down again, close to my chaff. I released more.

Above us, only three missiles remained. Debris rained down, whether from a ship or the station, I did not know.

Sam took aim and shot a missile.

I dropped more chaff and turned back toward the city again and considered what Sam had been through with Taft. "I understand. It was an impossible situation. It still took me ten years to forgive them. I had to almost escape first."

Sam shot at another missile. "Tell me about escaping."

The *New Delhi* used its railgun to destroy the last actual spy ship—which was scorched and damaged. Apparently, my gambit to get them to shoot each other had worked at least somewhat.

Once the real spy was gone, the three remaining freighters promptly surrendered. The destroyers ordered them into orbit for boarding.

The last missile exploded on the chaff.

It was over.

We'd saved the city and the colony, but not the space station. Airini and Varick had been up there. Damn. Nor had we saved Jackson. Double-damn.

I sighed and flew a bit farther before I turned to head back to the city. Why did winning feel so bad? I took the *Revenge* down. Not wanting to face the authorities, I opted to go back to Vada's house rather than the spaceport.

As soon as we landed, Vada and the children emerged from the house and waited for us. I lowered the ramp then jacked out of Virtual Vision. After clambering up out of the pilot's chair, I stopped to stretch. It felt like I'd been sitting there for a week.

I leaned down to help Sam to her feet then clasped her shoulder. "Good shooting, Tex."

She laughed as she took her helmet off. "It felt good in a lot of ways."

Together we went out into the corridor to collect Taft.

As Sam, Taft, and I walked aft to get to the ladder down to the cargo deck, it felt like the weight of the sky was pressing down on me. "I really don't want to answer any questions from the authorities right now."

Taft chuckled and took Sam's hand. "We're old. We'll tell them we're too tired."

We climbed down the ladder to cargo. I paused to check on Earl while Sam and Taft headed on down the ramp.

I peered over his stacked equipment. He was still lying on the padded hammock. "Earl, we're headed down for food and sleep. Care to join us?"

Earl got up but shook his head. "I think not. There is food here. I wish to work on what the sunstones do, if we will not be flying for some time."

I leaned on a molecular analyzer, still feeling bad about what I'd done to him. "I hope not. Let us know what you find."

I turned and jogged down the ramp after Sam and Taft. They weren't that slow, either. I caught up just as they reached Vada, who stood near the front door with Gamila, and the kids, Tamara, Dural, and Damien. No Detective Bossen, or any other officers, and, disappointingly, no Razzy.

The kids swarmed around us, bundles of energy and excitement. Vada kept watching the sky as if it might fall on us all. My chaff was floating down, scattering across the ground.

At last Vada pointed upward and tried to talk. "What...? But..."

I nodded, weary. "Yes. The space station is gone. I didn't think it needed protecting. Apparently, the destroyers didn't either."

Forlorn, she waved at the sky. "But Tamara's father was...doing training on genetics. And he..."

Vada threw her arms around my neck and sobbed on my shoulder. She held on. I patted her back, unsure what to do.

Tamara chased her brothers all around, screaming. It almost sounded like she was playing. Almost.

At long last, Gamila stepped up and laid a hand on Vada's arm. "Vada, should we feed our guests or send them elsewhere?"

Vada lifted her head. "What? Oh. No, we can't send them away." She turned and headed to the door. "Kom in, everyone. We'll get you some food."

"And then we need sleep," Taft said.

Vada smiled and slipped her arm into his. "Of course! We have extra dream rooms."

I wanted to hug Gamila for distracting Vada.

Dural dashed past us then stopped in the doorway to show us a big handful of chaff. "Momma! Momma! Look what we found! It fell from the sky like rain!" He turned and ran into the house, trailing chaff.

Sam broke up laughing. "You glittered the town!"

★ ★ ★ ★ ★

My dreamtime had me chased by missiles while running through mountains of glitter as I hunted for elusive sunstones. I woke with the feeling everything was taken care of—we'd won, beat the Romans again! Except we still didn't understand why. What were the Romans after? What did the sunstones do?

Sam, Taft, and I ate breakfast—toast, poached eggs, and bacon—which I mostly pushed around on the plate, lost and directionless. I had no idea where to go next or where I would find a home, back to where I'd been before Jackson Conscripted me. Everything was done. What was I going to do now?

Well, at least I knew how to occupy the next few hours. Sam said I needed to experience the game complex, so she and Taft led me in that direction.

When we walked out the front door, Vada was sauntering down the *Revenge*'s ramp. For a moment my hackles went up. No one got on my ship without permission! But Earl and Roberre were there, and she had such a smile on her face. Plus, figuring all the spies were gone, I hadn't locked the ship.

I squashed the anger that tried to raise its head and waved. "Hi, Vada. We're off to the game complex."

She fairly bounced down to meet us. "Good idea! Have fun. I'll be down in an hour or so." Then Vada went on inside.

As Sam and Taft started around the house, I stood staring at the *Revenge*. "What was Vada doing on my ship?"

Taft laughed.

Sam poked him and rolled her eyes at me. "I think Vada partook of one Earl Montague Cristo while we slept. He *is* a fine-looking man."

I walked backwards, still staring. Why was I competing with Vada for my men? Why was I possessive of Earl? "But...but...I haven't gotten so much as a *look* from him!"

Sam laughed and thumbed at the ship. "Did you ask? To bed him, I mean."

I frowned. "Um...I asked him to lunch."

She took my arm, turned me around, and guided me past the house on a path toward the game complex. "Earl is rather literal. If you want him, you need to tell him exactly what you want. I'm sure Vada did."

That made so much sense. Not that I wanted to hear it. Still, it made me consider what I did want. One night? A series of nights? A relationship like Sam and Taft had? A home. That's what I wanted, a home, and that meant with someone, with family, whoever that might be. How did one create a family?

A family with Earl? I did a stumbling pirouette as I tried to see Earl inside my ship then resumed the walk to the complex. "Well, he is a lot more interesting now, not to mention dangerous."

When we rounded Vada's house, a vista over the game complex opened before us. It sprawled. The path we were on led to a side entrance on the twilight side. The parking areas were off to the north, toward the city.

I paused to consider the enormity of the place.

Sam let go of Taft's hand and pointed to the left, away from the city. "There are three basic areas. The job skills area, where you compete against people in like careers. Winners have their pick of jobs." She pointed at the area farthest away. "The athletic area, which is all pure competition. Track, weightlifting, gymnastics, and the like. And closest is the social section with music, dancing, chess, games, and that sort of thing."

The complex of buildings, stadiums, tracks, and more. "What is all this for? I guess I understand the jobs section."

Taft answered, one arm raised like an orator, like Ambassador Retts. "When the *Sydney-Copenhagen* arrived at Eksil and all saw the planet where they had to live, many despaired, for they had neither food nor fuel to reach another star. Captain Alinta, smallest in stature and largest in wisdom stood before the assembled. "I have walked this place in my dreams and seen our children and our children's children. Here they will thrive. Here we will play games as we have on this long journey, games that will teach us who should do each task. Thus, the best and the brightest will lead us to a glorious future."

He sounded like the ambassador. I cocked my head. "School here must be interesting."

Moreover, with passengers and crew from Australia and Denmark, places where athletics and competition were considered an integral part of life, they would indeed have played games on the long journey.

Sam smirked. "I would not know."

Taft pointed off toward the jobs section. "Game jets first?"

After taking his hand, Sam led us down the hill. "Later, my love. Burgundy needs to tell me her story, so social games first." Then she took my hand, too, offering comforting warmth. "Tell me more about your anger. Justified, I might add."

I gathered my thoughts and told her about the first trip to New Hebron, Goldblum's Flying Circus, and almost drowning. Then, how I'd hacked into the administration computers. "And there was no source for my scholarship. Just everything paid."

Sam snorted but took my hand and Taft's at the same time. "Sloppy. They could have at least put in a fake billionaire with a scholarship."

I hadn't considered that. "Maybe they wanted me to find out. If so, I think they regretted it."

We arrived at the game complex's side entrance, which interrupted our conversation.

Taft opened the door and held it for us. Then Sam led me into a clean, bright corridor with murals of what could only be life on the *Sidney-Copenhagen* and its perilous journey to Eksil painted on all the walls. Offices of some sort lined the left side wall, and the aroma of food—baking cakes and fried meats wafted toward us. The nearest room on the right, about twenty meters down the hall, explained the wonderful smells. It was a cafeteria, where maybe a hundred people sat talking and eating.

Sam and Taft both stopped and took in the crowd. At last Sam frowned. "Oh, dear. This is so much quieter than usual. Everyone feels the loss of the station."

It seemed noisy. Perhaps normally people were boisterous here. Perhaps I was used to living alone on a spaceship. I felt like I'd failed them all.

I frowned. "Maybe we can be the entertainment today."

Sam clasped my shoulder. "I'd rather be invisible. Come on."

Past the cafeteria there were a series of rooms with six or so tables setup for board games of various types. Sam picked a room with only four other people playing a card game I didn't recognize. There she picked a table and set up to play chess against me.

As she moved her white pawn, Sam looked me in the eye. "What did you do next, with your anger?"

I smirked, considering my own black pawn for a moment before moving it forward too. "I found out how much I could get away with."

Then, as we played, I told her about how I'd buzzed the graduation ceremony, and how I'd not been charged with anything at all.

At that, Taft shook his head. "She's your sister, all ret." He waved away southward. "During the chase phase of her first gold medal, before I ever met her, she took her plane through the needle's eye in Ny Nitmiluk Gorge."

I wanted to see this needle's eye, maybe fly through it. Maybe later.

Sam shrugged and imitated the plane with her hand, first level, then sideways. "I needed to lose him. And if you turn a VTOL jet sideways you can...go strange directions"

Taft wagged his finger at Sam. "That's how I know you're related!"

Sam slapped at his hand, laughing. Then she turned and winked at me as she moved her queen out past her pawns. "They really didn't charge you at all? With anything?"

"Nothing. That's when I knew I had to go through to get out. Make them think I was at least going along. Of course, that meant..." I stumbled over the next part. I'd had to leave Hiram behind.

Sam nodded with a sad, regretful frown, and laid a hand on mine. "That meant *Hiram's Revenge*. What did you do next?"

Next? Oh. I snorted and got my king's rook into play. "I didn't buy a ticket for the liner. I just got on. Then I demanded a suite and ran up ridiculous bills. Never paid a cent."

Sam guffawed, hand over her mouth as she took my pawn. "Burgundy! And that didn't warn them off?"

I shrugged and moved a knight over to protect my rook. "Apparently not. I took the grav-bus to the Clark Academy, without applying."

I went on to tell her about all the pranks I pulled, and the special instruction with Jackson and Cinti, right up until my solo flight when the drives cut out and I figured out the sabotage.

Sam came to her feet. "They did *what?* I'll *kill* Cinti! That's unconscionable!"

I waved her back to her seat. "Cinti apologized later for not defying the orders she'd gotten. And I did make it back. I just took an extra day or so doing it."

Somewhat mollified, Sam resumed her seat and folded her arms.

I opened a hand and sacrificed my bishop to take her knight. "They should have known by then. I got my revenge." I told her about graduation day, at least *my* graduation day, and how I'd destroyed the campus.

A slow, evil grin grew on Sam's face while I told the tale. At last, she snorted. "They deserved it." Then she snorted. "Ha! I couldn't have said that when I was an admiral."

That she was listening meant so much. I already liked my sister, but she cared. That she agreed with me meant even more. My heart warmed as I told her about the aftermath, Jackson, and my job offer.

She gave me a solemn nod. "He was right, you know. That was a hell of a piece of flying."

Both of us paused then, Sam holding her queen in the air, as we remembered that Jackson had just blown up. She set her queen on the black square near my last pawn so softly it made no noise.

I slammed my knight down to block her bishop. We'd whittled each other's pieces down to where neither of us could do much and the game was about to be a draw. "How can he be gone? And in such a stupid way?"

Sam shook her head. "Draw?" She picked up her king. "If that ship hadn't been on the ground out in the dark at a hundred below zero, I'd think he'd escaped and left the beacon so we could find the ship."

She was right, except if he'd escaped, he would have found a way to contact us by now. It was possible to survive at those temperatures, if one was prepared, but how would he have prepared for that while being held captive? I still didn't want to believe he'd been on that ship.

I pointed toward the twilight. "I suppose we could go see."

A man stepped up to the table. He had hair dyed blue to match the pin on his shirt collar. He might have been lingering, waiting for us to finish. "Might I have the next game?"

Sam opened one hand to indicate it was my choice. I wanted to finish our conversation.

Taft got a gleam in his eye as he resisted a smile. "Why don't you show him your card."

At Taft's suggestion, I pulled the card from my pocket and held it up in two fingers.

My potential chess partner blanched. "Oh! I'm sorry. I didn't mean..." He turned and fled.

Sam and Taft laughed, and a man walking by shook his head, joining the mirth.

The newcomer said, "In over his head." He bowed with a grin. "I, however, am not so faint of heart, if you desire an opponent for chess or any other game."

I waved the card at him. "Are you sure? It's a scary card."

The stranger grew serious. "It is indeed a scary card, but just the ret amount scary for *me*."

His slight emphasis indicated his superiority over the prior stranger. Something odd was going on. My card had gold trim. This man's pin was bronze, with one silver, and two bronze triangles.

Somehow these two strangers brought back the hubbub of voices around us, since there were now another eight people playing games in this room. I'd been concentrating on my sister so much that I'd tuned it all out. I wanted to go back to the illusion of quiet.

I gestured at Sam. "I need to finish my conversation with Samantha here. Perhaps later."

A new voice said, "And I'm afraid I need to talk to all of them."

Razzy stepped up beside the stranger and laid a hand on his arm. Then he nodded at Sam and Taft.

The stranger started in surprise and bowed to Razzy. "Of course. Excuse me, sir."

And he left too which almost disappointed me. I'd been about to figure something out. Then Razzy smiled at me, and suddenly some flirting banter sounded nice.

I gestured to a nearby chair. "Well, if interrupting important conversations is your thing, have a seat."

He pulled a chair over and sat between Taft and me. Then he winked and spread his hands. "You have made one completely and helt false assumption that a conversation without me is important."

Taft nodded sagely, eyes twinkling with mirth. "The man has a point."

I rolled my eyes. "Yeah, but he's going to ask us about the battle, and that's yesterday's news."

Razzy cocked his head. "And today's news is?"

I tapped the chessboard. "That Sam and I battled to a draw, of course."

Razzy gave me a grave nod. "I shall inform the Råd. In the meantime, it appears the Roman spies did have nukes."

I deflated. He just had to get real. I reached out and laid a hand on his. "I'm heartbroken. It never occurred to me they would target the station. I'm sorry."

Razzy sighed and covered my hand with his. "The destroyer commanders think the spies wanted a distraction. And apologized as well. Moreover, the Råd does not blame you or the destroyers for the station. Still. These spioner thought getting rid of the population was worth it for whatever the sunstones can do."

Sam started setting up the chessboard again. "Don't forget they are risking starting a third war with the Council of Planets."

Razzy's eyes narrowed just a fraction as he regarded Sam. "It's a big risk. But why? What are they getting?"

I gestured back up toward Vada's house. "Earl is working on it. I hope he'll discover something by tomorrow."

With that, Razzy stood and offered his hand. "I believe that covers all our business. Would you care to dance?"

I wanted to do both, talk to Sam and dance with Razzy.

Sam reached over and smiled as she patted my arm. "We can talk later, unless you need to leave."

I stood, held out my hand for Razzy. "I think I'll stick around at least a few more days." I didn't have any place to go or anything to do, after all.

Smiling, Razzy took my arm and led the way out of the game room. Sam and Taft followed. Back out in the hall,

Razzy found a stairway and down we went. The stairwell walls were painted in a burnt umber and amber in a geometric pattern that seemed altogether too bright. Before we reached the bottom, music throbbed on the air.

We emerged into another bright corridor, cerulean blue now contrasting with the amber, and painted instruments emitted rainbows of visible sound. The first few doors along the way appeared to be tiny concert venues. About half were closed and had faint music that reached the hallway.

Farther down, three open rooms had dance floors, though not many people. Each had a different style of music playing. Razzy walked past two rooms with boisterous, bouncy music and chose one with a soft but insistent rhythm. Five men, one of whom was the second stranger from before, who was not afraid of my card, and three women danced in couples. Six musicians, three women and three men, played on a small stage. Everyone except Sam and Taft were my age or younger. There was an eerie instrument I'd never heard before, but it somehow harmonized well.

Since I'd already agreed, Razzy led me out on the floor. Only then did I realize I didn't know the steps. Only then did the other couples' dancing, sinuous and high stepping, in and out of each other's arms reach my attention. Only then did I realize I was out of my depth in more ways than one.

Sam and Taft went and stood along the left wall near a water cooler, just watching.

I laughed. "I don't think I can do this."

Razzy winked. "It's not so hard. I'll teach you."

He moved around behind me and took an elbow in each hand. His body was warm against my back, causing me to flush. My face grew hotter still when he started swaying to the rhythm. He put his feet next to mine and showed me how to move them.

All the women in the room stared, even the ones in the band.

It didn't take me long to learn the steps well enough not to fall on my face. I was relieved and disappointed both when Razzy moved around to dance in front of me. Then again, I hadn't anticipated how erotic the full dance was, with Razzy getting so close, and both of us thrusting with our hips.

Sam and Taft, giggling like school kids, joined the dance, and it changed the whole tenor of the room. It was just so cute and touching to see a couple in their 80s doing this dance. Smiles dominated everywhere, and they also took some of the attention away from me.

When the song ended, Razzy and I stood breathing hard for a bit, and went to get some water from a cooler over by the door. Sam and Taft joined us, laughing and smiling.

However, when Razzy led me back out onto the floor, the stranger from before stepped up and bowed. "Might I have this dance?"

I turned to Razzy and gestured to the newcomer. "If you want to dance with him, be my guest."

Razzy shrugged. "Sure. Why not?"

When he stepped forward, the stranger sidestepped and gestured at me. "I meant you, with the scary card."

Now I rather had to dance with him, although Razzy interested me more. "Very well. I'll probably survive *one* dance."

I walked out on the floor with him as the music started, and noticed his former partner, a woman wearing a gold pin with gold, silver, and bronze triangles, had absconded with Razzy. She looked both relieved and excited.

Her expression made me readjust why the women had all been watching me. Did they all want to dance with Razzy? Probably. He *was* a Rådmand, after all.

When the steps started, I stayed just a little farther away from the bowing stranger than from Razzy.

I found I had a question and pointed at his pin. "What is the significance of those pins?"

"Oh! I thought everyone vidste." He pointed at the pin and the three triangles in succession. "The setting is a person's genetic potential, and the stones are game performance. Social, physical, and job skills."

My stomach sank. I didn't want to know this, since it came so close to comparing me to Brandy. "So my gold card is genetic potential. What makes it so scary?"

Again, my question seemed to puzzle him. "It's the distance between. Everyone tries to breed upward, but blue to gold is too great a reach."

I stopped. Hands on hips and scowling. "Breed! I'm not breeding with anyone!"

Everyone stopped. Staring at me. I stomped off the dance floor to the water cooler where I drank and fumed.

Sam made her way over and gave me a quick hug. "I'm so sorry. I should have warned you. I've just gotten so *used* to it all."

Her words and touch calmed me and got my brain started again. A raft of clues fell into place, like Vada's three children.

With a groan, I walked out into the corridor. The air seemed cooler out there. Sam followed, but no one else. I leaned against the wall and summed up my realization. "When the *Sydney-Copenhagen* arrived here, they were desperate for people, and they needed the most competent. Being practical, they disconnected childbearing from any kind of permanent relationship, and both parents helped raise the kids, but separately."

Sam nodded. "Yes. There are often homes with multiple people, both adults and children. Ones like me and Taft are rare for the young and more common in the aged, people living together for companionship."

"And this?" I waved at the whole game complex.

That put a smile on Sam's face. "Everyone comes here to practice and to get laid. Having children is hugely important."

Oh, lord, my behavior was completely wrong. I pointed back to the room. "So what I just did was..."

Sam laughed and shook her head. "Shocking. Almost unheard of."

I rubbed my temple. "Do you think Razzy will talk to me again?"

"He's probably the only one who will." She pointed back at the room with her thumb. "I'm going to tell Taft, then we'll go out to the track. We can walk and talk there."

A few minutes later, we walked through more social areas, and then past gyms and courts of various kinds, all with people practicing or performing for potential partners. Then we stepped out into the perpetual sunshine. There, a small stadium sat around a dirt running track. Some impromptu races were going on, men and women, where the winners paired off. More people about to get laid, based on the snippets of conversation as we walked by.

Sam pointed to a trail that led back through some trees that appeared planted just to shade the path.

We skirted the track and headed into the makeshift woods. Sam took my arm and patted my hand. "Now, where were we? Oh, you'd just graduated by destroying the academy."

I took a few steps and reoriented my thinking away from sex and faux pax's. "I went to work for Pauley Spaceways. It was a decent job, but I spent my time saving up for a ship. Then Cinti showed up and apologized."

I told her about her buying *Hiram's Revenge.*

Sam snorted. "My money. I approve. And I can forgive Cinti too."

After that, it was the emotional escape and how I became a freelancer out of Angel's Planet. Sam whistled when I described it, from the atmosphere to the smuggler's mentality. I skipped my early jobs and got straight to being hired to break Eksil blockade and how I'd modified the *Revenge.*

When I got to Jackson showing up just before I left, Sam stopped dead in her tracks. "He said *what?*"

I stopped and turned back toward her. "Um, he said, 'I knew you'd be in on this, Burgundy.'"

"That son of a bitch!" Then she started swearing like, well, like a freelancer from Angel's Planet.

Puzzled, I put my hands on my hips. "What? What did he do?"

Sam shook her head, then paced one way and the other. She slapped a tree trunk beside the path. "It's exactly what Jon said to me when I first met him. I don't think I've told that to a soul. Rachel was there, a few others, I doubt anyone else would remember."

I thought back on the biography I'd read. Jon had been her first love, lost like Hiram, except he'd died. But no such introductory statement had been in that book.

I leaned against the tree trunk next to her. "But why does it matter?"

Shaking her head, Sam started up a little hill. When we reached a bench under a tree, she lowered herself onto it like an old woman, as if she'd aged a decade in a few seconds.

I pushed off and followed, standing in the path, waiting for whatever was going on.

She shook her head, a tear in her eye as she looked up at me. "I'm wrong. I must be wrong."

I sat down next to her and laid a hand on her shoulder. Her reaction far outstripped what I'd been talking about, and any significance I could see. "What?"

She closed her eyes. "First, the panel that blew to kill Jon shouldn't have blown. Not like that. Then, Jackson always felt familiar to me, like I'd always known him. And we never became lovers. He always refused. Then he used the exact words with you that Jon used with me."

"I don't understand."

"What happens if you take *Hiram's Revenge* straight up in Lu Space? Or even over backwards?"

Before I could answer, my bracer beeped. Earl's voice said, "Captain, I have something."

Sam climbed to her feet and gave me a hand up. When I started to object, she waved it off. "Let's go get Taft and Rådmand Balbuk. What Earl found is important. I'm just a senile old woman who had her heart broken as a kid."

Senile? Not that I'd seen, but I let it go.

✶✶✶✶✶

Thirty minutes later, I walked up the ramp into *Hiram's Revenge* with Razzy, Sam, and Taft in tow.

On the walk over, Razzy had managed to lean close and apologize. "I'm sorry. I made assumptions I should not have made."

I grinned and bumped his shoulder; glad he was still talking to me. "Only half of your assumptions were wrong."

He laughed and touched my hand. "Perhaps I should retire to my hus and contemplate which half that might be. Would you care to aid me in my contemplation?"

I rubbed my chin. "I may be able to assist with such an endeavor."

Especially since I had an uneasy feeling about their culture, but I couldn't say what yet. My back-brain was still working on it. Telling my tale to Sam had distracted me from it, plus Romans and star sharks and sunstones.

As we walked up the ramp, Roberre and Earl appeared at the top.

Sisters' Homecoming – 104

"Woof," Roberre said, while Earl stood tall, silent, and menacing.

Razzy, Sam, and Taft all paused a moment, having seen Roberre's handiwork, not to mention Earl's, against people who broke into my ship.

I continued up the ramp. "Hi, Roberre. Hello, Earl, how are you feeling?"

Earl started to speak, then frowned and laid a hand on Roberre. "I remember being...someone else. Dante. I was Dante, a spy, I think. I do not want to be that person again, but I would like to remember more."

Sam stepped up and laid a hand on Earl's shoulder. "There are people who can help with that, back on Earth. It may not be a pleasant experience."

Earl gave Sam a solemn nod. "It is not very pleasant now. Quite confusing."

I laid a hand on his shoulder, conscious of what Razzy was hearing. I'd wanted a new job. Perhaps helping Earl to make up for breaking him was a first step, "I will fly you to Earth, if you want to go." I would be able to seduce him on such a trip, if I dared. If I wanted to. For the moment, I gestured farther into the ship. "Now, show us what you found."

Earl nodded. "Yes, Captain." He headed back into his little testing area up beneath the bridge.

The four of us followed. Earl had four machines setup with sunstones mounted in them, and a neutrino catcher, which was related to how gravity drives worked. You had to warp space to catch neutrinos.

Earl picked up a computer and swiped a presentation up to the wall. "First, as expected, sunstone chips can be used as light NAND gates, from which all logical operations can be derived. Given that knowledge, I concentrated on energy focusing and transmission."

He swiped a graph up to the wall, and I stepped forward, examining the lines and numbers. Did that mean think what I think it did? I pointed. "Antimatter?"

Earl ticked the point off on his fingers. "Yes, Captain. It can be used both to assist gathering antimatter and as a focus for an antimatter reactor."

Had we just solved the how to get faster ships conundrum Pauley Spaceways had had me try so hard to fix?

Taft was utterly baffled. Sam and Razzy weren't much better, glancing between the two of us for clues.

I put my hands on my hips, figuring I would explain later. "What's the power curve?"

Earl swiped another graph up to the wall.

In my time at Pauley, I'd studied ship engine power curves every day for almost three years. None of them resembled this. "Holy Lu space, is that eight gs with compensation?"

Earl nodded. "Yes, Captain. The fuel will be expensive for some time."

Sam gasped. "Eight? That's...almost worth the effort the Romans put into keeping it secret."

Expensive fuel might mean dual reactors, only using antimatter for boosts. Still. I wanted to outfit *Hiram's Revenge* immediately.

Razzy folded his arms and turned a stern visage to Sam. "Samantha Kastanje, how is it you know about Romans and gravity ships?"

Sam's shoulders slumped a moment, then she straightened up and faced Razzy. "Might as well get it out. I came here thirty years ago after a distinguished career out there as a star pilot. If anyone finds out I am here, you will be overwhelmed by people trying to find me."

"What?" Taft took a step back, shocked again. "Why? I thought you were an admiral?"

Sam turned and kissed Taft. "I'm full of surprises. I got rather famous before the admiral thing."

I snorted. "Rather famous is an understatement," I addressed Razzy. "She's right. You would be inundated."

My back-brain perked up. Inundated! That was it. What would an invasion of people do to Eksil's odd culture? My thoughts coalesced and my heart sank. Eksil was in trouble and didn't even know it.

Frowning, I rubbed my scalp. "But there's something you haven't figured out yet. I'm sorry, but when that first trader found you all those years ago, it destroyed your culture. The games, genetic potential, breeding upward, none of it will survive."

Sam groaned and reached out for Taft's hand. She leaned against him. "She's right. It hadn't occurred to me. I was too busy trying to be local. For now, I suggest leaving the port closed."

Razzy glanced back and forth between the two of us. "But why? I don't understand. What will they do to us?"

I spread my hands. "Nothing. There are just billions of them and thousands of different ways to live. It may take a couple generations, but enough people will come who, like me, don't want to play. People here will make other choices. Eksil citizens will also leave, like Ambassador Retts, and see how people live out there. When they come back, they won't be the same."

Razzy's face fell, eyes white with fear, but he kept his composure and turned to Sam. "Why keep the port closed?"

Sam, holding Taft's hand, turned the other one up. "To give yourself, ourselves, time. Send out ambassadors. Bring ambassadors here. Learn what the rest of human space is like. Then, together, we can decide what we will be when we do open the port again."

Razzy cocked his head. "We?"

Sam stepped closer to Taft, holding onto his arm. "We."

Razzy ran a hand through his hair. Then he walked halfway down the ramp. The rest of us waited in tense silence.

At last, Razzy came back up. "I hear you. I will take this to the Råd. We may need to send to Earth to ask Ambassador Retts if she agrees."

On the last, he met my eyes, so I nodded. "I would be glad to take a message. I appear to be going anyway. You will need more ships to protect the system from Roman raiders. I suspect the star sharks come here for sunstones, too. Those stones may be all over the system. I could also help negotiate contracts to sell the sunstones."

He bowed to me. "Good. Takker dig. I finde I need to go." Then he winked at me. "But I will return for our deep contemplation of my assumptions."

As he walked down the ramp, I took in his hair, his shoulders, his legs, and his ass. I had not felt like this about a man since...since Hiram, except maybe with Earl. I turned and fell into Sam's arms.

She stroked my back. "What's wrong, sis?"

For a moment, I just breathed. It had been a long journey since the moment I'd kissed Hiram goodbye. "It's just...I haven't felt like this about anyone since I left Hiram. And now I'm free enough that I can contemplate appropriate actions. But he may not want more than a little contemplation. And it's just..."

Suddenly I felt silly, but after all these years, I still missed Hiram. Maybe because there hadn't been anyone else. There might be Earl, but even he didn't know who he would be when he was healed.

Sam stepped back and laid her hands on my shoulders. "One step at a time. You're free from those bastards who created you, and you can *contemplate* with one of the most desired men on the planet. First things first, just talk to him. Remember, he came back after what happened down there." She pointed toward the game complex. Then she grabbed Taft's arm and held him close. "Also remember, I met this lug when I was almost sixty. You have time."

I pressed my lips together. "Time."

Then I noticed Earl, who stood silently by the wall, watching. He wore his normal, placid expression, but I read more heat behind it than had been, and that made me blush.

"Um, Sam, should we finish our conversation?" I considered where and gestured to the ladder. The common room would do. Earl did not need to hear this.

Sam gave Taft a quick kiss. "Can you go see if Vada has any food for the bunch of us?"

I walked over, then gestured for her to proceed me to the ladder. "Though why I'd want to talk to a senile old woman is beyond me."

She snorted. "Well, there's one more thing I remembered, so maybe not so senile."

Then she didn't speak until we reached the common room. I used my bracer to fold the table into the floor and the couch out of the wall. The two of us sat.

I shifted to halfway face her and put an arm across the back of the couch. "What did you figure out?"

She gestured back toward the ladder. "That little conversation reminded me that Jackson not only told me how to get *here*, but he gave me a file with what to expect from the culture. The game and everything. And it had files to set up an identity for me."

I shot to my feet, crossed the room and back, three steps each way. "How the hell would he know that?"

Sam fidgeted, tapping the couch seat. "Damn good question. At the time I was depressed and desperate, so it just seemed a little odd. However, if Lu Space can be used for time travel...well, it all seems ridiculous. I just had my heart broken like you did as a kid."

I sat back down and took her hands. "Sis, that's an awfully big leap from a chance phrase and advanced knowledge of Eksil."

She gave me a self-deprecating grimace. "Senile. But we might be able to test some part of it." She thumbed toward the bridge. "But assume I'm right. What do we do about it? It means Jackson may have survived."

Taft hollered from below that Vada had food ready for us.

As we rose, Sam took my hand again. "Also, Taft and I want you to come live with us. Would you like that?"

I beamed and lunged to hug Sam. "I would love that. Love it!"

I could live here? With my sister? More friends who were old, but I had Razzy and Vada who were my age, maybe even Earl, since he couldn't go back to Planeta De Angel. If I negotiated the sale of sunstones, I'd likely get a finder's fee, maybe even one for negotiating for Eksil to buy ships from Pauley Spaceways. For a while, at least, I expected I would fly Eksil representatives around the Council of Planets. A job, a place to live, a family. I even had two men to choose from.

I whispered in Sam's ear, "Let's test your straight-up idea, or going backward, whatever that means."

Sam pulled back to look in my face. "You will be fun to have around. Just what I need in my old age, excitement."

I had a ship, so I could still visit my parents, not to mention Cinti and Joyce. They might want to come here and so they could meet Sam, if Sam agreed. After the long journey to escape and live in exile, I at long last had a home. A home with my sister!

The End

ACKNOWLEDGEMENTS AND DEDICATION

Please remember to leave a review for this book at your favorite retailer.

This book is dedicated to Daniel Ashlock, who was a friend, college roommate, and fellow lover of science fiction and fantasy.

Visit my web site at:

http://www.richardfriesen.net

If you like my stories, consider becoming a patron to help me with the costs of editing and cover art. You also get early access to stories and inside information on what I'm doing:

https://www.patreon.com/richardfriesen

Clark Family Legend

The adventures of a family tied together by their love of space exploration...their cocksure attitude toward life...and their ace flying skills! If you love Golden Age SF writers like Robert A. Heinlein…first contact with alien stories…and genius pilots out to save the galaxy…the Clark family is for you!

<u>Prodigy's Loss</u>

<u>Ensign's Renown</u>

<u>Ace's Anguish</u>

<u>Student's Fury</u>

<u>Deuce's Exile</u>

Like superhero stories? Answer this: how can falling asleep be a superpower? Narcolepsy's opponents, and friends, and anyone who happens by, find out quickly and regret it.

<u>Narcolepsy Falls Asleep</u>

<u>Narcolepsy is Shocked</u>

★★★★★

Look for my epic fantasy series, **The Dreaming King Saga** in your favorite online bookstore now. Remember: he who dreams of the kingdom is king.

<u>The Tower of Dreams</u>

<u>An Uncivil War</u>

<u>On Black Mesa</u>

<u>The Gates of Heaven</u>

★★★★★

These professionals did wonderful work on this book:

Editing: Mia Kleve

MRK'd Up Editing

★★★★★

Cover Art: GermanCreative at Fiverr.com

★★★★★

This is a work of fiction. Any resemblance to people real or imaginary is unintended.